Inevitable

A Hotwife Story

By Matthew Lee

Chapter 1

Aaliyah spooned the last of the vanilla ice cream onto her tongue, closing those pouty lips around the lump of sweet sugary delight. I should know better than to watch her mouth. In all our years of marriage I've gotten two blowjobs. I remember them well. They are enshrined in my sex-with-wife hall of fame. Ali needs to be wildly aroused before she'll do something as nasty as take my penis in her mouth, and that was only after I'd showered first. Alcohol helped both times.

You pee from that thing, she'd said. *And semen tastes terrible.*

"Waiter," I said, raising a finger. "More wine."

He acknowledged me with a nod and hurried for the kitchen.

Ali eyed me suspiciously.

"Trying to get me drunk?" she asked.

"Maybe. A little."

She opened her mouth to show the lump of dessert melting in there.

"Bet you wish that was you," she teased, causing a little drop to escape and run an inch towards her chin. She laughed and clamped her lips shut and I laughed too.

Maybe more wine wasn't needed after all.

We were celebrating Aaliyah's birthday and she looked smashing. She'd recently voiced concerns about getting older and her fading beauty, but to me she looked better than ever. Tonight, she'd worn a clingy electric blue satin dress and I knew that meant she subconsciously sought male reaction. She'd gotten plenty. Every now and then she needed a boost and the wardrobe would shift towards revealing more skin. Early in our marriage I'd noticed and said something and she'd acted like I was crazy. She'd given birth to our son, Archie, eighteen years ago but you saw no trace of that pregnancy in her body now. She'd kept the swollen breasts but diet and exercise had narrowed the waist and slimmed the thighs. To see her in her bikini, you'd struggle to guess her age accurately. The wine arrived and the waiter poured our glasses for us. I raised a toast to growing old together.

"I'll go kicking and screaming every step of the way," she said.

I took a sip but she downed most of hers. The waiter had moved on to the next table but I noticed him looking at Ali. I realized from his angle her dress gave a delicious shot of cleavage.

"Don't look now," I said. "But you have an admirer."

Aaliyah sent her eyes casually around the room, catching the young man in the act. Ali knew where his gaze fell. He looked away without realizing he'd been seen.

"Well that was flattering," she said.

"He got a long look."

"I forgive him because he's cute."

"I forgive you because it's your birthday," I said.

"Please," she said, wagging a finger in the air. "You don't have a jealous bone in your body."

I raised my hand as if swearing on a Bible.

"That's not entirely true," I said. "You've made me jealous several times over the years. Remember Cabo?"

She giggled.

"I blame the wave," she said.

"You didn't exactly hurry to put your top on again."

"It was a topless beach, David."

"You were surrounded by hot young local men, all of them gawking. Topless beach had nothing to do with it."

"It was a nice moment," she chuckled.

I let it go. We talked as we finished our meal and paid the bill. Ali wasn't drunk but had a lovely buzz going. She held my arm as we walked around the lake taking the long route back to our car. The night air was warm and carried the scent of honeysuckle.

"Put the top down," Ali said as we arrived at our black Audi R8 convertible. "The weather is lovely."

I did as she asked and minutes later we were driving through the fiscal district high rises. The wind whipped around, flipping and puffing her dress in wonderful ways. I caught a glimpse of blue lace panties. Men never outgrow certain things. She gazed at the scattered nighttime clouds and let herself feel the moment.

"I'm going to have a hard time with wrinkles," she murmured.

"You'll always be beautiful to me, Baby," I said. "Wrinkles are still a long way away. You're gorgeous, Ali, especially tonight."

She smiled.

I stopped for the light and her dress settled across her legs, exposing toned thighs almost all the way up. She looked down and so did I.

"Tennis pays off," I teased.

At the next light, I turned left and immediately encountered stalled traffic. Construction cones and flashing lights guided us all into a single lane. After fifteen minutes, Aaliyah pointed down an alley.

"Can we cut through here?" she asked. "Catch Broadway and then the freeway?"

I shrugged.

"It's worth a shot," I said. "We'll be stuck in this for more than an hour."

I cranked the wheel and left the main road. Nobody followed me.

The alley was poorly lit and took us deeper into downtown. Our chance to hit Broadway was ruined by a warehouse. We detoured around it, seeking a way out, eventually following whatever road opened before us. We quickly found ourselves in a bad area, clusters of dangerous men dotting the occasional corner. I stopped at the next light and a skinny man wearing NBA Lakers shorts and a T-shirt waved at us.

"You looking for fun?" he asked Aaliyah.

His two companions laughed.

"I got a ton of fun right here, Angel," he continued.

He hooked his thumb and pushed down the front of his shorts, revealing a long, thick, dark penis, with large balls hanging low. His pubes were bushy.

"Jesus Christ," Ali said to me, rolling her eyes. Then, to him: "Real classy, asshole. Does that work for you? You score a lot of women like that? Fuck off."

He laughed at her insult.

"You'd love it, Mama. All you high class ladies do. Try Alfredo's big dick, Baby. You'll see. I'll make you cum like fireworks."

The goddamn light would not turn green. His friends were dying laughing. Alfredo lifted his penis, balls and all, and offered them to Ali, waving them like a bouquet of roses for her to smell.

"Once you go Fredo," he joked. "You never go back."

"That doesn't even rhyme, you idiot," one of his friends laughed.

Ali shook her head like she was deeply disappointed in the man.

"Come on, Baby-Girl," he pleaded. "You are super-fine. I promise you'll love it."

Ali looked away but then faced him again, staring at the man's exposed penis before meeting his eyes.

"You are shockingly immature," she stated.

The light turned green and I accelerated away. I was angry, wishing I wasn't outnumbered, wishing I could have gotten out of the car and beat his ass bloody.

"I'm sorry, Baby," I said. "That was ugly."

She shook her head.

"The alley short-cut was my idea, David. Just forget about him and his stupid friends. Don't let them ruin our perfect night."

I hit a few greens and then stopped at the next red.

"I feel a little light-headed," Ali said.

She slipped a shoulder out of the seatbelt and lowered her head to my lap. I stroked her soft hair and when the light turned green, continued up the street. I felt her shift a few times, getting comfortable, but I was in no way prepared when her hot mouth enveloped my penis. I don't know how she got me out without me knowing, but that didn't matter. All that mattered was her swirling tongue and vacuuming maw. I gave myself a mental high-five for ordering that last glass of wine.

I slowed the car. No way would I end this too soon. Ali sucked my penis like it was made of candy and I did not question her. The warm air billowed under her dress, caressing her skin and exposing lovely flashes of bare flesh. I was hard and throbbing in her mouth for the third time.

I slid a hand over her shoulder and scooped under to lift a fat and weighty breast. She filled my hand, soft skin squeezing between my fingers. Her hard nipple rubbed against my palm. Her soft moan floated up to me. I saw Broadway ahead but that wouldn't do now so I cranked the wheel again and entered another alley. That led to a one-way street which took me back to the warehouse. I turn onto the street we'd recently left behind, savoring Aaliyah's slow and sensuous mouth. I wasn't thinking clearly, obviously, as driving while getting blown fully occupied my mind. It took all my concentration to obey the speed limit and stay in my lane.

Alfredo awaited us at the next red light. For an instant, we didn't recognize each other. Then the lightbulbs went off.

"Where's your lady?" he laughed, stepping closer to the car. "You drop her at home? I don't do dues, my friend."

He and his friends started to laugh but then the wind lifted a yard of electric blue dress into the air. Three pair of eyes looked over the passenger door to Ali head-down in my lap.

"You brought her back to me!" Fredo chuckled. "And warmed her up, too."

Down went the front of his shorts again. He was close enough to our car that he flopped his cock and balls over her door, hanging his penis over her foot on the door rest. If there'd been no car in front of me I would have run the red light. Ali finally realized the voices she heard were close and sat up quickly, back against her door, mashing Fredo's dick. She recoiled, unsure what warm spongy thing touched her, and turned to see what she'd hit.

His dick was inches from her face.

"Go ahead," he boasted. "Give it a kiss."

I was out of the car instantly.

"That's it, motherfucker," I growled, enraged. "That's too far. What the fuck is wrong with you? Put your nasty shit away. You always wave your dick around? Fucking animal."

I was coming around the trunk when his friend stepped off the curb and planted a fist hard on my jaw. I wobbled but stayed on my feet. He tried to hit me again but I ducked and landed one on his cheek. He staggered backward. His buddy joined in and I found myself facing two on one. I landed a few good shots but they landed more. The scales tipped rapidly.

I'm no trained fighter. I haven't fought since high school. One thug darted behind me and grabbed my arm. Before I could free myself, the first guy knocked the wind out of me with a shot to the gut. The man behind slipped an arm around my throat. I was in serious trouble. I was about to get choked out.

"Stop it!" Ali shouted. "Leave us alone."

"You came back looking for trouble," Fredo said. "Pull up with a dick in your mouth. What you think would happen? Of course we all want some, Mama. You fine as fuck."

"Just let him go," Ali pleaded. "We'll leave."

The two guys let me fall to the ground on my ass.

"Your man started that shit," Alfredo said. "Don't blame my guys. They were just defending themselves."

I focused. Fredo remained at my wife's door, his penis and her face filling the same frame in my vision, his penis far too close to her. The street light turned green. The car in front of ours drove away.

"You want to leave?" Fredo said. "Okay. No problem. But you start throwing punches and think we're just gonna turn the other cheek? Think we're just going to take your shit? No dice. We should stomp your ass into the sidewalk." He turned to face Ali. "But we're not going to do that. Mama, all you got to do is kiss my dick and you can go. You and your man. No hard feelings."

I started to get up, ready to fight again. Fredo's friends held me. One socked my ear. The other put his boot on my chest, forcing me down. Aaliyah looked at Alfredo's penis hanging in her face, her expression pure disgust.

"You guys came back and started all this," Fredo continued. "All you had to do was drive away. You laid hands on my boy, Reggie, and I can't let that slide."

He turned his hips towards Aaliyah.

"Go ahead, Darlin. Give it a smooch. One kiss and you can go."

I was on my feet but unsteady. His buddies held back, watching crazy Alfredo lay down the law. They looked ready to bust out laughing. I glanced around but nighttime streets in this area of town were empty.

"Aaliyah," I said. "No."

I got socked in the ear again.

"Let's just get out of here, David."

"Let him up," Fredo ordered.

They did. I rose to my feet and one of the guys slapped my cheek. I staggered towards the driver seat. I saw one of Ali's tits had slipped free from her dress. Alfredo stared at it like a wolf. Ali lifted his long cock with fingertips and aimed him at her mouth. Time slowed. My wife leaned in and planted a full, lip-mashing kiss on the head, just above his pee hole. He reached down and tucked her breast back into her dress. Ali froze at his touch, his palm cupping her smooth tit and sliding her into place. I'm sure it was just my mind fucking with me, given the extreme emotions of the situation, but I swear her lips remained planted a half-second longer than necessary.

"Not so bad, right?" he chuckled, pulling his cock away from her. "Now we all have something to remember this night. Get the fuck out of here."

He dropped his substantial cock into his shorts and snapped the elastic waistband into place against his flat stomach. Ali stared at her hands in her lap. I dropped into the driver's seat and shut the door. Fredo leaned across Ali to slap my cheek, hard.

"Never come at us like that again," he warned.

The engine was running so I put the car in drive. The light had turned red again but with no car in front of me, I drove through the red light.

We rode in awkward silence.

"They would have beat you," Aaliyah stated, finally. "Badly."

"I know. I understand what you did. Sorry I lost my cool."

More awkward silence.

Minutes later Ali lowered her head to my lap again. My zipper was still down from before and her warm, wet lips slithered around my meat. The earlier blowjob had been spectacular but it paled in comparison to this. Emotions were high. Aaliyah poured her heart and soul into sucking my dick. Was she trying to make me feel better? Was it guilt over kissing his dick? Was she just horny from the wine? Did this count as my fourth blowjob or was it a continuation of the third?

I don't know. What I do know is that I felt the love and adoration my wife has for me through her oral worship of my penis.

I freed her fat tit again and caressed that plump mound and my wife moaned from deep arousal. She forced my dick to the back of her mouth and sucked hard, tugging on the semen stored in my balls. This was like nothing she'd ever done before.

Wine or the relief of terror passing or the return of fear of aging: I didn't give a shit. Her mouth was Heaven. I warned her I was getting close but she just groaned and sucked harder and faster. I couldn't hold back.

"Now!" I grunted.

She whipped her mouth away and her hand took over, stroking my slimy dick like a piston. I swerved in my lane, ejaculating hot sperm on her neck and chin. One blast landed across her face. One splattered her ear. I groaned as I shot, flexing and bumping, my butt writhing in the driver's seat.

"Goddamn!" I growled.

Ali giggled. I shot over and over, each time a little less until I was drained and wiped out. She tucked my penis in my pants and worked the zipper up. She straightened in her seat and wiped my goo off her face, adjusted her dress and leaned her head on my shoulder.

"What a night," she said after a long time.

"I'll return the favor when we get home."

"You better believe it. It's my birthday. I should be driving while you go down on me. You're such a lucky husband."

"I tell myself that every day," I said.

Chapter 2

Archie was awake when we got home so we chatted for a minute before bed. He noticed a spot on Aaliyah's dress. She said it was a spill from dinner.

"You should have worn a bib," he said.

Ali flashed me a knowing smile.

"I should have," she agreed. "You're right."

We did not talk about her kiss on Alfredo's penis. Both of us acted like that moment never happened. The next day I toured clients through a new listing and had fantasies of driving by Alfredo's corner and gunning him and his friends down. I checked Google Maps to fix his location in my head. Violent day dreams are not usually my thing but fuck that guy.

My clients weren't thrilled with the house so we headed to the next. I got home around three and Archie had exciting news.

"It's the drone racing championship," he said, shoving a brochure in my hand. "August. Muncie, Indiana. We have to go."

I glanced at the pamphlet.

"I'll pay for everything," I said. "I told you get straight A's and that's what you did. I'll make all the arrangements."

"Yes!" he cried, pumping the air with a fist. "I gotta tell Mark and John."

He turned towards his room.

"Wait," I said. "Where's Mom?"

He pointed at the backyard.

"Pool," he said.

Off he went. I sauntered to the backyard.

Aaliyah lay stretched on the chase lounge, her eyes hidden behind sunglasses. AirPods pumped music into her head as her olive bikini top struggled to contain her tits.

The bottoms rode high on her hips. Her body gleamed from sunscreen and sweat. Ali works in hospitality and her appearance is a big deal. She signed a contract with weight restrictions. That's all well and good until years pass and you start to age a bit. Now the pressure to look good sucks. I ogled a minute before opening the sliding glass door.

I stood over her. To answer her question how my day went I complained about my clients and that I'd need to take them out again. She invited me to join her on the other lounge and soak up sunshine.

"That sounds good," I said.

I jogged to the bedroom, changed quickly into trunks, grabbed two cold beers on my way through the kitchen, stepped onto the patio, and dropped onto the offered chair. I sat her beer on the low table next to her and took a sip from mine. Her head was resting comfortably, face aimed at the gorgeous blue sky, so I took a moment to gawk at her again. I am a lucky husband. I told her about my plans to take Archie to the drone championship.

"That sounds delightful," she said. "I'll have the house to myself for a week. What a treat for everyone."

"I thought you'd say that."

Around the corner the side gate clanked. The pool guy, Roscoe, stepped through with an armful of equipment and waved. I waved back.

"Roscoe's here," I said.

Aaliyah didn't budge. I tapped her foot and she removed an Air pod.

"Roscoe's here," I said again.

"Oh good. Make sure he tests the water and doesn't just clean. The tiles are getting water spots."

This bikini was one of her smallest and I expected modesty to kick in. Roscoe is an older friend of Archie's, graduating last year, and I thought Ali would cover up in front of a family friend. Nope. Roscoe started his own pool service business while a senior and we hired him right away. It was Archie's idea but Roscoe has done a fantastic job. We've known him since he was five.

Sometimes I can be truly dense.

Aaliyah knew exactly what day and time Roscoe treated our pool. It was the same every week. If she was out here in one of her tiniest bikini's when he arrived, that was planned.

A hot wave rushed through me. Ali *wanted* Roscoe to see her like this. Was this more growing-older insecurity? Probably.

"I need to set up a home search real quick," I blurted. "Back in a minute."

Ali offered pursed lips and I gave them a peck, heading inside and then watching through the reflective glass. They couldn't see me but I could see them. Archie was in his room and we wouldn't see him again until dinner. Roscoe stacked his pool equipment and dipped a plastic tube into the water. Ali turned her head ever so slightly. The sunglasses hid her eyes but I knew she watched him now. Roscoe stretched and tugged his shirt off over his head, casually tossing it to the lawn. The young man was cut: lithe and lean. He dropped the skimmer in the water and began walking slow laps. As he approached my wife, his head turned on a pivot. Ali pretended to be asleep but I watched the controlled rising and falling of her chest. His eyes crawling her skin thrilled her. Jealousy tickled the base of my brain but faded. This was Roscoe: silly, goofy Roscoe. I only saw him as a neighborhood kid, not some sexual threat.

Ali continued her charade of obliviousness by pinching her bikini top and tugging the fabric lower. I was a foot away through the glass and noticed she'd exposed the tiniest edge of darker areola. She made the same move to the other breast. Roscoe stared, burning the sight into his memory. I was a young man once. He'd be jacking off to that sexy sight later. Maybe he had a girlfriend. I imagined him insisting on a blowjob while picturing my wife.

Nothing happened for a while. He skimmed and cleaned and she sunned. The next time some task brought him to this side of the pool Ali shifted, partially sitting as she adjusted her lounge to lie on her stomach. For a moment, she was on all fours, heavy tits hanging behind a top that barely held on. Then she settled and reached behind to untie the knots at back and neck, brushing aside the strings. Roscoe gawked at all that bare skin and bulging breast. I wondered how many times this drama had played. We were a month into summer. Ali had been lying by the pool for weeks. Something told me she always timed her sunbathing with Roscoe's arrival.

I heard Archie's bedroom door open so I returned to my lounge chair outside. Ali and I chatted about silly life details until I heard her breathing deepen. Roscoe finished and waved goodbye and I let myself nap too.

Chapter 3

The skill level was insane. The course filled an arena, pitch dark, hoops and gateways illuminated by black light. The audience watched from the bleachers as these master drone pilots flew an intricate obstacle course at breakneck speeds. Each drone carried a camera and the views were broadcast on a massive split screen. I was astonished by the talent and lightning reflexes.

Archie knew several of the competitors, including a few cute girls and one with blue hair, so I let him mingle with his people. He'd come by to check on me but I was fine. The competition was enthralling. When we weren't enjoying the games, we wandered the town and ate at different restaurants. We enjoyed quality father-son time. I checked on Aaliyah with phone and text several times but she was keeping busy with work or relaxing by herself at home.

Days passed and the field narrowed. Quarterfinals became semifinals became championship round. That also meant Sunday, pool day, was approaching again, only this time husband and child would be out of town. Would Ali alter her behavior? With us removed, would she dare more?

Sunday arrived and I was distracted as the top two contestants, a young man and a young woman, battled for first place. I sent a text to Ali just before Roscoe would arrive her time and received no answer. I sent more, telling her I loved her and asking how her day was, but only silence greeted me. I put that worry aside and watched the final match as Charlie, the young woman with blue hair and a friend of Archie's, won the top spot.

Archie invited Charlie to dinner with us to celebrate and she accepted so I offered to pay. At dinner, I learned blue-haired Charlie was in Muncie by herself as she was estranged from her family because she was gay. Mom and Dad announced homosexuality was a sin and stopped talking to her. How a parent can turn their back on their child boggles my mind.

Charlie lived a county away from us back home and used to attend a rival high school, her years overlapping some with Archie, which is how they originally met, before she dropped out.

"Now I just move from competition to competition," she said, "always placing first, second, or third. I have a roommate back home but the prize money lets me jump from event to event. It's pretty cool."

It did not sound cool to me, it sounded lonely, but I kept my opinion to myself. I did swap numbers with her though. My heart went out to her. If there was some way I could improve her situation, I would.

"I think pictures by air would really help sell a house," I told her. "I'd like to pay you to sometimes photograph and video certain listings for me. Interested?"

"Hell yeah," she said. "Extra money is always good."

We finished dinner and I suggested Archie and Charlie hangout together while I went back to our hotel room to call Ali. I waved goodbye as they headed down the street. After a minute, Charlie took Archie's hand. Cute.

At the hotel, I called and Ali finally answered, apologizing and explaining she'd fallen asleep by the pool. I pictured her lying there in the sun and a sudden inspiration hit me.

"Topless?"

She giggled.

"Wow," she said. "How did you know? Were you spying on me?"

"No, but with me and Archie out of the house I thought you might let yourself enjoy all that freedom."

"I did. It felt wonderful."

"Bottoms too?"

"In for a penny."

I paused a moment to picture my nude wife basking in the warm sun.

"Are you picturing me naked right now?" she asked.

"Yes."

"Is that a pleasant thought?"

"Ask my hard dick."

"I wish I could. Nude sunbathing turns me on. If you were home, I'd help you with your problem."

"If I was home I'd fuck you on your lounge chair."

That hit hard. I heard Ali draw a sharp intake of breath. She loved the idea.

"We'd need to keep an eye out for Roscoe," I added. "Sunday is his day. I hope he didn't come by while you were naked and asleep."

Tense silence. I could almost hear the gears turning in her head. I sensed her surprise at me making that connection. Now she had to pick a path and stick with it: admitting if Roscoe came by or not and admitting if she was aware he had or not.

"Oh my gosh," she said. "You don't think he saw me like that, do you?"

So. She'd decided on the innocent route.

"Is the green inflatable float still in the pool?" I asked. "He always sets it by the barbecue before treating the water."

"It's by the barbecue."

"Then I'd say he came by while you were sleeping. Lucky boy."

Aaliyah said nothing, and that confirmed she'd been awake for Roscoe's visit. If this was truly news to her she'd freak out. One of Archie's young friends seeing her naked? Such an event would have left her mortified. She should be talking a mile a minute, questioning if it could be true, wondering what she should do next, doubting she could ever face him again. Her silence spoke volumes.

"I guess I should be more careful," she said at last.

"Or not. I'm sure the man enjoyed the view."

"You think? This body is not too old for a young man like him?"

At last the truth emerges. Ali was testing her own attractiveness, seeing if she still had what it takes to turn heads.

"I've noticed how he looks at you," I said. "He's probably jacked off eight times by now. I remember what it was like to be his age and see a gorgeous naked woman."

"Now I *really* wish you were home," she purred.

I regretted my wife and I had to play this game about what was happening but I understood her needs. It was harmless, Roscoe no doubt loved it, and Aaliyah ended up horny. Honesty would be better but that meant openly confronting her insecurities and that's always scary. I decided to just let her have her fun and play her games and get the confidence boosters she needed.

"Me too," I said.

The conversation shifted to the drone competition, the fun Archie and I were having, and what a delightful friend Charlie was.

"We'll be home tomorrow afternoon," I finished. "Then I have to take Eve and Sonny out again first thing in the morning."

"Ugh."

"Yes, I wish they'd make up their minds."

Chapter 4

Charlie sipped her non-fat mocha latte with four extra shots of espresso and contemplated my offer.

"Archie won't know?" she asked. "Archie can never know."

"No one will know. Only you and me."

"Spying feels wrong."

"It's not spying. I know what my wife is doing. I'm not trying to catch her so I can divorce her. I'm trying to participate in a way that won't freak her out. It's complicated. She's too embarrassed to come right out and tell me her needs. This way I can see what's happening and make sure she's safe."

Charlie thought about it again.

"I guess that makes it okay."

"Is the money good? Do you need more?"

"No, you're paying me a lot. I can't take more for such a simple job and I already own the cameras and lenses I'll need for distance shooting. The picture will be like you're standing next to her. It just feels so sinister, you know?"

"I get that but trust me, it isn't."

I knew my argument was weak but hoped the money was enough to put her over the edge. A moment later she gave a hard nod.

"Awesome," I said. "How does it work?"

She withdrew her phone and tapped buttons for a minute. When she finished, my phone chimed.

"I just sent you a link," she said. "I'll set everything up and then text you an alert before I start filming. Follow that link and you'll be able to watch everything on your phone or home computer. There will be no sound."

"I don't care about sound."

She shrugged.

"We'll see," she said. "If they talk I think you're going to wonder what they say to each other. I hope this doesn't turn ugly. If it starts to, I'm out."

"That's fair. I promise it won't."

We finished our coffees and talked about life and I ended liking her even more. She'd been through a lot but remained kind. She wore baggy clothes but when her clothing pulled tight I saw enough of her body to know she was shapely under all that. Too bad she was gay. I thought she'd make an excellent girlfriend for Archie. They were such great friends.

The rest of the week dragged. I was so excited for Sunday to arrive everything else was annoying. When Archie informed Ali and me he'd be gone all day, I added I'd be out all day too, showing houses.

"Another day to myself?" Ali chuckled. "Perfect."

Friends arrived for Archie around nine and we waved goodbye as he headed for the lake to waterski. I kissed Aaliyah at the front door, pretending I had a booked calendar. I risked asking her what her plans were, worried I'd jinx myself.

"Soak up some sun," she answered. "Work in the garden after."

I drove away.

Twenty minutes later I sat in the same coffee shop where Charlie and I had met only days before. I was holding my phone and looking at the dark screen when it chimed. I opened a text from her and touched the link and my backyard filled the screen. The drone was so high Ali was a mere pink dot on a green background. A tiny pile of yellow was her unused bikini by her chair. I was about to text Charlie to get closer when I saw Roscoe's truck pull up to the curb in front of our home.

I had to set the phone on the table. My hands trembled. My dry lips stuck together. I sipped some coffee to wet them and marveled as the steady picture zoomed. Charlie was a wizard. Gay Charlie was also distracted by naked Ali. As the picture drew closer, Charlie veered over to check out my naked wife. Ali was on her back, adjusting the towel behind her shoulders. If she was aware Roscoe had already pulled up out front, she didn't show it. She looked delicious.

Charlie's text floated in the corner before fading: *Your wife is a babe!*

I didn't answer. Answering would mean closing the picture for a minute to switch to text messages and I wasn't about to do that. Ali settled onto her lounge and relaxed, pretending to sleep. Charlie gawked at my nude wife for a moment and then zoomed out, showing Roscoe crossing our front lawn to the side gate. He moved carefully, carrying less than usual, trying to stay quiet in case Ali was nude again. Charlie and I watched the young man closely. Ali's head jerked towards some sound Roscoe made but then she controlled herself, forcing herself to lie still.

She knows, Charlie texted, zooming in.

He eased through the gate and approached the back corner of the house. He peeked around, using a tall cypress as cover.

Score!

He set a skimmer and bottle of chlorine down and leaned against the stucco, openly staring at my gorgeous naked wife. Charlie zoomed out to get Ali and Roscoe in the same frame and then zoomed in as close as she could but keep both. Roscoe was rubbing the front of his pants.

I know how he feels, Charlie texted.

Ali, fully aware Roscoe stared, pretended to stretch and shift in her seat. Her legs parted, her ankles moved to each corner. She opened herself to his probing eyes, wanting to show him everything. Charlie couldn't help herself and zoomed in on my wife's neatly trimmed pussy. I knew Ali was aroused because her inner lips, normally hidden behind her labia, protruded slightly, like a leaf of lettuce between hamburger buns. I waited for Charlie to zoom out again but she didn't, mesmerized by my succulent woman. I wondered if she was masturbating to Ali too.

Finally, the camera moved to capture Roscoe and Aaliyah again and we discovered the young man had lowered his zipper and held his naked erection, slowly stroking. He'd draw his fist up to roll around the head and then back to his baggy white pants, stroking the length over and over. I waited for some comment from Charlie about disgusting penis but she said nothing, even zooming a little so we saw his dick better.

Movement drew my eye to Ali again. She'd realized what Roscoe was doing and wanted a better view, but had to appear she was still sleeping. She rolled her head and smacked her lips and shifted slightly, allowing her to see the young man clearly. Nothing like some hot young stud jerking off over the sight of you naked to boost the ego.

This is so hot, Charlie texted. *I don't even like dick but this is hot.*

I jumped to text messages and risked typing a quick reply: *God! Isn't it?*

When I got the picture back on screen Roscoe now braced himself against my house, stroking his dick with purpose. He was determined to cum. Ali's lips had parted and her skin seemed to glow. Her inner lips were swollen. I knew when I got home she'd jump me. I might even get a rare blowjob out of it.

Charlie showed why she was a master. Instinct guided her and she zoomed on Roscoe at exactly the right time: a long white cord of ejaculate blasted from the tip of his penis to glitter in the sun before falling to my lawn. He followed that with another and another. Damn those youthful testicles. Even Charlie was impressed, texting a *Goddamn!* as she held the camera steady. To her credit Ali's behavior revealed nothing. To someone that did not know her as well as I, she seemed asleep. But I knew better. I saw the wild tension in her legs and back. I saw the taut strain in her face and the corners of her mouth. Sexual frustration saturated my wife down to her bones.

Roscoe finished blowing his load all over my grass and then zipped up, backing all the way out the gate. He clanged and clattered as he filled his arms with supplies and then banged some more at the gate. Ali quickly covered herself and entered the house. Roscoe got to work as if the backyard had always been empty. I sent Charlie a text stating that would be all for now.

Dude, she replied. *I can't wait for next Sunday.*

Me either, I shot back.

I closed the website and dialed Aaliyah.

"My clients canceled," I said. "I'm headed home."

"Good," she grumbled. "I fell asleep in the sun again and had a sex dream. I'm horny. Come home and fuck me."

"Who about?" I teased. "George Clooney? Brad Pitt?"

"Just get your ass home," she ordered.

I downed my coffee and drove. She greeted me at the front door, wearing a bikini but not the yellow one she had with her earlier. I moved to kiss her but she broke it quickly, dropping to her knees to free my dick. She jerked it for a minute and realized I'd get hard faster in her mouth so in I went. She didn't even need me to shower first, which staggered me. I did indeed get hard fast. I gazed down at my dick in her mouth for only the fourth or fifth time and marveled at her excitement. I loved seeing my dick in her mouth.

I didn't understand it then, and I wouldn't understand it for a long time, but I was unknowingly modifying my own behavior. Subconsciously I recognized that turning my wife on by any means resulted in hot sex for me. I would eventually come to understand but by then it would be too late, too late for what happened.

She stood and faced away, pulling her bottoms aside, ready for penetration. I decided to make her wait and knelt to bury my face in her pussy from behind first, sliding my wiggling tongue into her drenched cunt. I was stunned by how wet she was. She thought about telling me to fuck her but then my tongue found her clit and she groaned. I ate until she came and then stood, slamming my hard penis all the way in. I held her ass in both hands and hammered her tight hole, fucking her wildly. To my surprise, and hers too, I think, she orgasmed again. That was good enough for me and I let my load rise, driven by her load moans and groans. When I started spurting, she clawed at my ass, ordering me to shoot her full.

Chapter 5

I am a selfish person. Instead of reassuring my wife about her insecurities, I catered to them. I encouraged her to dress sexy when we went out, drawing the attention of other men and feeding her need. My bouts of jealousy were a small price to pay for the remarkable sex life I soon enjoyed. Over the years Aaliyah had mentioned several men at work that consistently flirted with her and my advice, my insistence, had always been that she ignore them. That changed. When she next came home with a story of office titillation, I asked her what he looked like, how she felt about his advance, if she found him attractive. Disguising my own desires as emotional support, I suggested she call his bluff and flirt back at him. I said she should turn the tables on all of them. I said there was no surer way to make them all behave. Pure rubbish when it comes to men, I know, but she took to the idea and their increased attention made her feel wonderful. She was horny every day. My suggested changes were subtle but combined they had a profound effect. She shared tales of office intrigue almost daily.

Sunday arrived like a freight train, barreling down on me before I was mentally prepared.

Archie spent Saturday night with his best friend and wouldn't be home until Sunday evening. I made sure Ali knew she'd have almost the entire day to herself. I was brushing my teeth Saturday morning while Ali showered next to me and through the beveled glass I realized she was shaving her pussy bare. Jealousy rammed stiff fingers into my guts but I said nothing because jealousy also grabbed me by the balls. What would Roscoe think when he saw *that*? I knew Ali was doing it for our pool guy and my body caught fire. My hands shook so much I had to concentrate to finish brushing. My dick swelled under my towel. I told her I needed to hit the road and she wished me well. I ran a few errands and actually showed one house before I drove to the coffee shop and settled in. Charlie sent the link early, as eager to see what would happen as me.

I had no worry Roscoe or Aaliyah would spot the drone. The camera was powerful enough to stay far away and there was plenty of sky for Charlie to maneuver. I tapped the link and the picture appeared: Ali walking out the sliding glass door already naked. Charlie zoomed right away.

She shaved! my co-conspirator announced.

The camera got closer. Ali's succulent cunt begged to be eaten. I could feel Charlie's excitement through the phone.

What if she fucks him? she asked with the straightforwardness of today's youth. *Shaved pussy means sex.*

I leaned back. The thought had never occurred to me. This was a game, a manipulated and arranged scenario which would result in hot sex for me. I had such utter faith in Aaliyah I never considered the possibility. She was only testing the attractiveness waters, not searching for a new partner.

She won't, I texted back, but my words sounded hollow even to me.

Charlie left it alone. We watched Ali move to her lounge and position it for maximum sun but also maximum exposure towards the side gate. My wife was boldly taking what she wanted. Charlie sent the drone high and I spied Roscoe's truck zigzagging through the neighborhood. He parked in front of our home as Ali dropped onto the lounge, stretching her long legs like a cat. Charlie zoomed as Ali slipped on her sunglasses and AirPods, settling into position. She ran her palms up and over her full tits before resting her arms off the chair over her head. Roscoe repeated his approach from before, sneaking through the gate to gawk at my nude wife.

Charlie's comment sizzled in my mind. The aim of boosting Aaliyah's arousal was to benefit me, not Roscoe. If his devouring eyes turned her on, fine. I was the one that enjoyed her extra excitement. I will have out-maneuvered myself if she cheats on me with him.

My stomach twisted like two alligators wrestling. I chewed a fingernail. I scrutinized the small screen on the table before me, watching every move either made.

Roscoe set his pool supplies on the grass and like before, withdrew his cock to start stroking. He was already stiff. Charlie zoomed for me and I saw the veiny spear slipping through his fist. We watched together for a minute and then suddenly Roscoe took a step backward. Charlie zoomed out and we saw Ali had sat up on her chair, acting shocked, covering her large breasts poorly with one arm. They exchanged words. Ali took a moment to think and then waved Roscoe closer. He hurried to her side, hard dick wagging.

Uh oh, Charlie texted.

The young man stopped a foot from my wife, maybe less. She leaned back on the lounge and lifted her arms again, accenting the gorgeous shape of her tits. They were talking, fast, nodding and occasionally laughing.

Aaliyah began to finger her pussy. Her free hand began caressing her breasts, teasing the nipples. Roscoe stroked with purpose and I knew my wife had asked him to ejaculate for her. He stopped long enough to open his pants and shove them to his knees and then he was at it again, thrusting his hips and jerking fast. Ali leaned closer, studying his body, examining his young cock. She leaned back again and spread her pussy with two fingers, pumping another finger in and out of her squishy hole. Her fat tits wobbled. Roscoe had a frozen expression of stunned disbelief.

Suddenly a long rope of sperm launched. Ali sat up, attentive, watching every young male muscle flex, every blast of hot cum sail. Droplets of sperm showered her breasts and thighs. Roscoe staggered, shooting the copious load of youth.

When he finished, my wife invited him to take the other lounge. My lounge. They talked, neither making any move to cover themselves. Roscoe drank her in like he wanted to remember this moment for the rest of his life, which I know he did. Eventually he stood and zipped up. Ali reclined again, casually returning to sunbathing. Roscoe got to work on the pool and Ali allowed him the pleasure of staring as much as he wished. Once he finished, he collected his supplies and exited through the gate. Charlie started to follow him but I texted her to stay on Ali. She did and we both enjoyed my wife masturbating to a toe-curling, back-arching, mind-blowing orgasm. After she caught her breath, she plucked her bikini from the lawn and walked inside the house.

That. was. HOT. Charlie texted.

I was shaking all over. I couldn't touch my coffee. I sat in my little corner of the coffee shop and watched the video again and again. She hadn't fucked Roscoe, but I knew the idea had crossed her mind. I *knew* it.

So what? What did I expect? I wondered if her orgasm had drained all her passion and I'd get nothing when I got home.

Nope. Far from it. Aaliyah was ravenous for my dick. We fucked in the kitchen, we fucked on the couch. She sucked my dick *twice*. We fucked until half an hour before Archie got home and then cuddled like teenagers the rest of the night. Archie commented how sweet our affection was. I told Ali she had permission to sunbathe nude wherever she wished.

"Be careful what you ask for," she taunted. "You may surely get it."

Monday morning, she dressed for work in the sexiest outfit yet. For her, anyway. She needed no prodding or encouragement from me. Archie was eating cereal at the dining table and complimented his mother on her appearance. She stopped dead in her tracks.

"I think that's the first time you've ever said that to me," she told him.

"Well, it's true," he countered. "You look really pretty."

That night, on the way home from work, she stopped and joined a gym.

Chapter 6

I watched the video again and again, picking out new details each time. To watch a young man, fully erect, walk towards your naked wife will burn a hole through your heart like Alien blood. I kept watching though. I kept watching because Aaliyah had never looked so sexy, so turned on and hot for sex as she did on that video. Seeing her like that turned me on too.

Ali informed me Sunday was now a workout day so I told Charlie she'll only photograph houses for a while. She said no problem. Ali soon complained about the gym and how hard it was to get a good routine going and I had the bright idea that she ought to hire a personal trainer. I caught myself before I said anything, buying time to see who was available and narrowing the choices to one man: Jace Goodwin.

Jace, who went by JC, had a Facebook page and an Instagram page and I studied both. He was always surrounded by hot young women. His body was sculpted bronze and his swim trunk bulge pronounced. I figured the man that all the women wanted was the best man to flirt with my wife. If he could have any woman he wanted but gave all his attention to her, she'd feel special. He'd turn her on and I'd reap the benefit. I paid for six months in advance and arranged for them to meet at the gym. I thought about suggesting he should flirt with her but waited to see if he did on his own. Aaliyah was delighted when she got home, kissing my face and lips.

"What do you know about JC?" she asked.

"Only what his Google reviews said. Apparently, he's the best. Is there a problem? Should I find you someone else? Perhaps a woman?"

"No," she answered quickly. "No. He's great. He's just very handsome. Like, *very*. Did you know that when you picked him for me?"

I shook my head.

"You know I can rarely tell when a guy is good looking. He has muscles and an excellent reputation."

She was thoughtful for a moment.

"You find him attractive?" I asked.

"Oh, yeah," she said, emphatically. "Every woman at the gym finds him attractive. I got some cold stares while we were talking. I think training with him will be fun but there will be some jealous bitches giving me the Evil Eye."

I smiled.

"That will only make it more enjoyable," I said. "Flaunt it. Push the envelope with him. Get our money's worth."

I just wanted her turned on and I didn't care how. Our sex life was much better these days. He could fill her belly with butterflies and then I'd fill her pussy with spunk. Who knows? In time, she might even swallow my load. Now that would be a night to remember.

She was still thoughtful.

"What's the problem?" I asked.

"He's gorgeous. He makes me nervous. His body is perfect. I feel stupid and clumsy around him."

"Give him two weeks," I said. "You need time to see he's just a man. Give it two weeks and if you still feel too uncomfortable, we'll find someone else."

She slipped an arm behind my neck and gave me a sultry kiss. I knew what she was really doing. She felt guilty about her level of attraction but confessing everything up front freed her. Fine with me. She didn't know I had ulterior motives too.

The first week was pure business. Aaliyah learned the machines and the free weights, finishing with cardio. She did come home horny each night, especially her second night at the gym with him, but she also came home exhausted. We tried sex but she was too tired.

The second week things got better. JC isolated various parts of her body and trained one part every few days. Ali had time to recover. Days later she came home and described how he had put his hands on her to teach perfect form. She was trembling from his touch. He'd run his big strong hands up and down her legs, over her back, down her arms, across her stomach. Each time she needed to place her body in a certain position, he was there, touching her, guiding her to perform the exercise correctly. She'd watched Roscoe masturbate right in front of her but this was different. This was a man, a rugged, handsome man, and he was *touching* her, and touch changed everything. She was ready to pop.

I pretended not to notice how jumpy she was and just pulled her into the bedroom. She came less than two minutes after my tongue found her pussy. I decided that was too fast and kept eating until she came again. After, she rolled me onto my back and sucked my dick, working me into diamond hardness before I fucked her. I was getting my dick sucked all the time now. We were fucking almost every day. Things were looking up.

Friday night she informed me JC would visit our place to tan on Sunday. Normally he used a tanning salon but the place was shut down for remodeling so Aaliyah invited him over.

"He'll be here about noon," she said, timid, expecting me to get upset. "I told him about our high walls and trees and pool and how it's the perfect place for privacy. I shouldn't have, it's not appropriate, but I just blurted it out. Sorry, Baby."

"No worries," I murmured. "I have clients that day anyway." My mouth was suddenly dry. "Will you join him?"

She tried so hard to appear casual and indifferent.

"Maybe," she said. "Probably. I haven't in a long time and my tan is starting to fade. Is that all right?"

"Sure. I'll work all day so why not?"

She quickly changed the subject to groceries we needed. My mind raced. I knew Sunday night I'd have mind-blowing sex. We talked for a while and then I excused myself to use the bathroom. What I really did was fire off a text to Charlie to make sure she would be in town to operate the drone. Her reply took two hours but she said yes. She was out of town now but would return in time. My balls tingled like mad. Anticipation of hot sex with my wife had my heart pounding. She'd spend an intimate afternoon alone with JC, both dressed in only a swimsuit. She'd be wildly horny by the time I got home. Guaranteed. I'll admit I felt a pinch of jealousy, but it was easy to ignore. It was a small price to pay.

Saturday, we all went to the lake for lunch. Archie brought a friend, Taylor, a good kid but terribly nerdy. They bonded over Magic: The Gathering, entering tournaments and building decks. The game looked fun but difficult.

Sunday morning Archie left the house early. I killed time before showering and telling Ali goodbye. My booth at the coffee shop was taken so I grabbed a table in the shade outside. Right on time, Charlie sent the link.

JC must have arrived early because they both already stood in the backyard talking. Aaliyah wore a sarong around her hips. Her bikini was a lovely crocheted number we picked up in Mexico. She held two tall drinks that looked like tea. Her bikini top was modest, one of the biggest she owned. Her large tits were almost completely covered. Disappointment weighed on me. If the situation was too tense, she'd pump the brakes and keep everything utterly professional. She was already nervous enough about him coming over that she'd dug out that ugly thing.

JC wore booty shorts but they were tight like a Speedo. He held his shirt in his hand, toned body gleaming. He wasn't big like a body builder; he was ripped like a model. Strong and fit, not musclebound. They pointed at the lounge chairs and the sun and the lawn, discussing the best place to sunbathe. JC plucked the heavy chairs like they weighed nothing and placed them side by side on the grass. He added a small table. Charlie zoomed. Ali set their drinks on the table and untied the knot at her hip. Her sarong hit the grass. She settled into her lounge and adjust her sunglasses. JC dropped his shirt and withdrew a tube from a pocket. He squirted something on his palm and dropped the tube.

He leaned over Aaliyah.

He placed his hand on her thigh.

He began to spread sunscreen.

Oh boy, Charlie texted. *So cliché, yet so effective. I feel like I'm watching a Black Hole Sun video. You okay?*

I did not reply. JC boldly slid his hands all over my wife's legs. Ali tilted her head back and remained motionless. JC squirted more onto his palm and confidently moved to her stomach. I saw the tension in Ali's body. This was way outside her comfort zone but she was unwilling to stop him. She felt guilty but his hands felt fantastic.

From her stomach, he squirted more and began coating the skin outside her top. Charlie thoughtfully zoomed closer and I saw his fingers dent the edges of my wife's spongy tit flesh. Ali lifted her arms over her head, making it easier, giving him broader access. Emboldened, JC worked up her neck and down each arm, standing over her with legs spread. His crotch was in her face and she acted unaware but I was sure behind those sunglasses she stared. His hands drifted to her tits again, making sure he coated everything, fingertips grazing under the edges of her bikini top.

Sweet Jesus, I could barely breathe.

She held out a palm and he gave a dollop for her face. He gave himself a glop and started on his shoulders. Ali motioned for him to lie down and then she did for him what he'd done for her, dainty hands traveling the lumpy and bumpy landscape of his muscular body. Ali took her time. When she got to the edge of his shorts she hesitated. Charlie quickly zoomed and we both saw my wife's fingertips glide under the fabric of his boxer brief swimsuit. Nothing scandalous, less than an inch, but she had crossed the same line he had. They were in sync, on the same page, pushing the same envelope.

At least that's what I thought, but then an instant later JC stood and spoke. Ali hesitated and glanced around our backyard. She looked at him again. Two heartbeats later she gave a hard nod. JC hooked thumbs and slid his trunks down his legs and stepped free, now completely nude before my wife. I gasped.

Holy Mother of God! Charlie texted, guiding the drone around for a frontal view, zooming on the most important object just revealed.

JC's soft, hairless cock sat like a dainty mushroom in the sun. A fat scrotum rested below. He looked smaller than me and smaller than most dicks I've seen. I felt a flash of relief but I didn't know why. My wife was still about to run her hands all over his incredible body, spreading sunscreen. She squirted and rubbed his legs, working her way up as he towered over her like the Colossus of Rhodes. Whether from her touch or the warm sunlight on his skin, his penis began to swell. Ali ignored his lengthening appendage, spreading lotion across his stomach, chest, and neck. He turned, offering his back, and she started at his calves and worked her way up again, covering every square inch. Finished, she made a little circular motion with a finger like she stirred ice cubes in a cup of tea. JC turned again, facing her once more.

His once small cock now hung as long as his hand from wrist to fingertip, like a fleshy banana aimed at my lawn, weighed down by a plump and swollen head. Ali did not miss a beat, examining his body, searching for spots she'd missed. She then boldly squirted a dab on her palm and wrapped her fingers around his dangling meat. I gasped out loud. Several people at nearby tables turned to check on me.

My wife began a slow and deliberate stroking of his dick. Her free hand cupped his balls, spreading the lotion there too. Her hands worked and a finger disappeared between his ass cheeks. I suspected she ran a circular finger around his anus.

Charlie zoomed the closest view yet and although a little blurry and shaky, I watched JC's cock grow hard in my wife's hand, climbing defiantly. The helmet head expanded, ridged veins rose.

That guy is HOT, texted Charlie the lesbian.

Ali spent entirely too much time on this man's penis. He was protected against sunburn, for Christ's sake. She pulled and tugged, intent on making him as erect as possible. Once his dick protruded from his crotch like a tusk, she leaned back, sitting on her heels to admire her handiwork. He was thick and long and veiny and gleamed from sunscreen. Ali smiled and laughed with delight.

Charlie zoomed out and we watched them talk a while, JC's cock intruding like a third person listening in. Then JC plucked the bikini string at Ali's neck. She remained motionless. Encouraged, he plucked the other strings too and soon her bikini top and bottoms hit the grass. They traded positions with Ali standing and JC crouching. He began a deep massage of my wife's large tits and firm ass. He coated everywhere, even running his hand between her legs. She clutched his shoulder to keep from falling, her legs too weak to keep her up. She looked ready to swoon. He finished and they stood naked in the sun, sparkling and glossy, eyeing each other's naked bodies.

They're gonna fuck, Charlie texted. *Call her. Say you're headed home early.*

Ali carefully took his cock in hand again. She caressed the stiff shaft, her hand gliding easily from base to head. They were talking but we had no sound. Charlie had warned me and she was right. What were they saying? Occasionally Ali would slide her hand all the way down and leave the shaft to cup his big balls, rolling them around, all pretense of sunscreen gone. Ali was so comfortable with her actions. Was Charlie right? Was my wife about to fuck JC? I was frozen with indecision.

Charlie zoomed out to get the best shot of whatever happened next and a dot of white at the edge of the frame caught my eye.

Wider, I texted. *Show me the whole yard.*

Boom. What I'd seen was Roscoe hiding by the cypress near the gate. It was Sunday and he'd come to do the job we paid him to do. Ali hadn't sunbathed in so long I'd forgotten all about her pool guy adventures. Now there was yet another witness to join Charlie and JC.

Zoom on Roscoe, I told Charlie.

She did, and what I saw horrified me. Roscoe had his phone up recording my wife stroking naked JC cock. In an instant, everything was out of control.

Back to Ali, I ordered and Charlie complied.

Ali sat on her lounge, JC standing over her, his erection near her face but aimed over her shoulder. My wife jerked his cock fast, played with his balls, clearly tried to make him cum. She gazed up into his eyes as he smiled down on her.

She's going to be so horny tonight, I thought.

I was jealous. I was worried. I was fearful I witnessed the loss of my wife, the end of my marriage. But more than all that, I was anticipating how hot our sex would be. I was sure something was wrong with my brain.

JC reached down to caress Ali's big tits, rolling her nipples. He pulled his dick away from her. He placed a hand on her chest and pushed her gently onto her back. He dropped to his knees between her legs. He lifted her thighs and lowered his face and my beautiful wife opened her mouth to moan deeply, grabbing his head. His writhing tongue was in her bald pussy, tasting my wife's flavor. She folded her calves across his broad back. He held her thighs on his muscular shoulders and cupped her ass in his hands, lifting her hips to his mouth, devouring his dripping pussy like a juicy peach. His body was twice her size, dwarfing her. She looked like a child next to him. He gripped her butt cheeks as she squirmed, feasting, pussy juice dribbling. She came hard, covering her mouth with a hand and screeching into her palm.

He gave her no time to recover, moving up her body to kiss her on the mouth, counting on her post-orgasmic bewilderment and confusion. His cock curved from his pelvis like a long fat ram, a scorpion's stinger poised to strike, aimed directly at my wife's sopping cunt. Her hands found his face and she kissed him deeply, too overcome with lust to do anything but respond. The head of his cock touched her clit and slid down, settling into the dent of her cunt. He pressed his lips to hers and that muscular ass flexed, sinking half his cock deep.

I was half a city away but I swear I heard her heartfelt groan. He pumped a few times, wetting his length, and then lifted his torso high over her. Her eyes were huge. He held her ankles and spread my wife wide, plunging his cock all the way to his balls. Her back arched on the lounge, she grabbed his broad shoulders. He fucked her with strong, deep strokes and then scooped her off her chair, holding her under her ass and fucking her while standing.

This is the hottest thing I've ever seen, Charlie sent. *I'm so sorry.*

The bastard carried my wife several steps, fucking up into her body as he walked around their chairs. She clung to his neck, circling his waist with her legs, forcing her pussy down to capture as much cock as she could. He returned to her chair but on the other side, lowering her to her back and grabbing her ankles again. He spread her legs as far apart as they would go, tightening her already tight pussy around his bulging cock. Her head snapped back and her mouth opened wide. My wife was having another orgasm impaled on his meat.

Jealousy ate me alive but there was no denying the raw sexual appeal of them fucking. She was stunning, breathtaking, real porn a thousand times hotter. I saw her as my wife and that part sliced me open, but I also, somehow, saw her as my wife getting fucked, and that was an erotic sight like I'd never imagined.

At last he straightened over her. He hammered her pussy and then abruptly withdrew, his hand taking over as buckets of sperm flew from his cock, showering her, spraying hot seed all over her naked skin. Ali rubbed his ejaculate in, smearing his semen to mix with the sunscreen.

Just like that, it was over. He stood panting and then ran his fingers through his dark hair. He moved his chair next to hers before dropping onto it. Aaliyah scooted her body close to his and stretched her long legs. She lifted his soft cock and pulled it across his leg until the head rested on her thigh. She left it there, her fingers curled gently around the shaft.

In moments, they'd returned to sunbathing as if nothing had happened. I saw their lips moving and I was sure they talked about what they'd just done, but their bodies were once more comfortable and relaxed. At the edge of the screen I saw Roscoe withdraw from his hiding place and return to his truck. He possessed a video I was sure would haunt us, but I'd worry about that later. For now, I had JC's fat dick and what it could do to my wife to worry about. Aaliyah seemed infatuated. I was sure once the magic of the moment drained away guilt would crush her but for now she relaxed with a gorgeous new lover.

I thanked God JC had pulled out.

Pulled out.

Zoom on his cock, I told Charlie.

The picture rushed forward. The man's dick had not returned to his previous mushroom state. Instead, the plump draped sausage remained puffy, spongy and partially erect, like it somehow knew it would be called upon soon. Charlie held the lens steady as I studied every inch of the man's weapon. That thing had been inside her like I've been inside her. JC had felt my wife wrapped tightly around him in the same way I do. He knew how she felt around his cock.

No, my concise mind corrected. *Tighter. He's much thicker. Aaliyah would feel much tighter around him than she did around me.*

Thanks for that.

The head was rounded and slanted back along the shaft, the pee hole larger than usual. The veins had retreated beneath the skin, waiting to rise when excited again. His cock was handsome. I felt strange granting him that distinction but it was true. Some are ugly. JC had a photogenic cock.

Ali suddenly rolled over and grabbed her phone from under her chair. She answered a call and spoke a minute, then hung up and began hurriedly talking to JC. On a hunch, I had Charlie zoom out.

Around the block I saw Roscoe's truck parked at the curb. He must have called to say he'd be late today, giving her warning he was coming. She didn't know he'd already been there and seen everything. The two lovers dressed quickly and entered the house.

Minutes later JC drove away. Minutes after that Roscoe parked at the curb and entered an empty backyard, cleaning our pool alone.

I texted Charlie that was probably all for today and she signed off. I killed time at the mall and replied to work emails at the food court, waiting until I'd calmed enough to go home.

Aaliyah was all over me the moment I stepped through our door. I hadn't known what to expect: Bold lies or tearful confession. She avoided both, hornier than I'd ever seen her. She ripped my clothes off and sucked my dick. I was surprisingly aroused for a man who'd just witnessed his wife cheat and I warned her what she was doing would make me cum soon. She moaned with heartfelt lust and sucked harder and faster. I warned her again but she was relentless. I tried to push her away at the last moment but she fought me, sucking my dick hard as I ejaculated into her mouth, my spastic hips jerking and convulsing as I performed a lurching dance. I'd never cum in a woman's mouth before. I had no idea it would feel that good. I howled, I yammered, I staggered and gripped her head, fucking her vacuuming mouth like a beast. She groaned with blinding desire and sucked harder, desperate for every drop. I almost wept. Her tongue was a whip, coaxing every drop I could shoot. I laughed insanely, blasting away down her throat.

She took the last of it but kept sucking. Pleasure rapidly became a strange kind of pain. I tried pushing her away again but she fought me like a tigress, forcing me to endure the agony. I stumbled out of the kitchen, balancing on counters until I reached the sofa, Ali still attached like a leech. She pinned me there with an arm on each side, sucking and bobbing. My dick screamed at me. The weird pain peaked and plateaued and I covered my face with both hands. I'd need to hurt her to make her stop and I would not do that. I was utterly soft but wildly sensitive. Buried in the strange pain was a pleasure so intense I could barely recognize it. I focused on that.

In time, my dick began to swell again. I was stunned. Pain receded and pleasure grew and her moans of triumph lit a fire under me. I turned hard. Steel hard. She sucked me erect and then pushed me down, mounting and fucking. She came fast, screeching like a banshee. I shoved her aside and climbed on top, bending her legs back, aiming my erection at her sopping hole. She grabbed my hips to guide me and I fucked her hard. I fucked her like I was punishing her for what she'd done, rebuking her infidelity. I went insane. I was a wild man, an animal, hammering my pretty wife until I exploded deep inside her, gushing semen. I shocked us both. When I finished, I collapsed on top of her and neither of us could move.

The problem with punishment is that once it is completed, you've got nothing to hold over them. The debt has been paid. The reset button has been pushed. Maybe not completely true, in this case, but how could I now say I knew what she'd done and be angry about it? She'd throw the sex we just had in my face. How angry could I be if I could get that hard and fuck her like that? Not once, which could be a fluke, but *twice*.

Complicating every thought in my head was the sweet, sweet memory of only moments ago, blasting my load into her sucking mouth. Yes, pussy feels better than mouth but to my mind, Ali sucking and swallowing was the greater erotic charge. I'd never forget that moment. I can't remember each and every time we've made love over the years but I'll never forget shooting down her throat.

I wanted more. A lot more. No way would once be enough. I wanted to blast a gallon of cum into her stomach every day until we died.

If I told her I knew about JC, I'd never have that experience again. Most likely we'd separate, probably divorce. Guilt alone would drive her to never touch me again.

I was stuck with my secret. At least for now.

Chapter 7

Words cannot describe our sex life after that day. Although the images of Ali with JC killed me, I said nothing, enjoying the benefit of Aaliyah's soaring lust. I saw the guilt in her eyes. Her terrible secret ate at her. But the rush was too powerful and besides, hadn't I been encouraging her to attract other men? Wasn't it me that placed JC in her path? It was, and I needed to be a man about what I'd done. However she rationalized her actions, there was no way she would stop now. In fact, she stepped on the gas. I was at a close of escrow with my clients when my phone buzzed. I checked the message: *Off work early and JC had a slot open. I'm going to get a quick workout in.*

My insides caught fire. I knew what that meant. I forced myself to pay attention to the transaction on the table before me but in the back of my mind I knew JC was about to fuck Ali again. I fought back a groan of frustration. The minutes ticked away.

My gut told me the moment she arrived at his place. I don't know where he lives but I felt it when he touched her. I felt it when they kissed. My body went weak the moment he slid his fat cock into her.

Thank God I wasn't signing anything today. My hands shook too much. I listened and gave advice and helped my clients through the signing, but my mind and my heart were across town, standing by his bed, watching. I ached, but that pain was balanced by the anticipation of hot sex tonight. It was terrible what she was doing but incredibly our marriage was better than ever. We talked and laughed all the time now. She was *happy*. The demons of encroaching old age had been silenced.

An epiphany rocked my mind: was this her first time since the first time? I'd assumed this was her second time with the man. Enough time had passed she could have met him many times. I felt the truth in the question and sent my mind backward. There had been many nights Aaliyah had been wildly hot for sex. Had she seen him earlier those days?

I shook my head to clear it and the escrow officer asked if something was wrong.

"Headache," I lied.

We all finished our meeting and I handed the keys over. We shook hands and then hugged and I wished them joy in their new home. We said goodbye. I jumped in my car and raced home, beating Aaliyah by ten minutes. I was horny as fuck. She came through the door, surprised to see me, wearing tight workout gear without a drop of sweat anywhere.

"I'm gonna hit the shower," she said after we kissed hello.

I grabbed her wrist and whipped her around to face me. Archie was at his job so we wouldn't be interrupted. She tried to deflect me, saying she was gross and needed to wash off but I didn't care. I moved in, peppering her lips with hot kisses. She broke, lust rising fast. I pushed her sports bra above her tits and feasted on her nipples. They were already red and swollen. I spun her around and shoved her yoga pants down over her ass and she struggled trying to stop me but failed. I pushed a finger into her sopping, faithless cunt. Had he cum inside her? My mind reeled. After watching them in the backyard that day I presumed they both understood the need to pull out. She was drenched. I couldn't ask the question without revealing what I knew so I crouched behind her and spread her ass cheeks. I saw nothing definitive, but she was soaked.

I buried my tongue in her.

I acted on impulse and perhaps it wasn't the smartest thing but the situation was intense and who thinks clearly at a time like that? I've never tasted sperm so I don't know what I was expecting. All I tasted was pussy. Maybe a little saltier than usual but sweat could account for that. She squirmed extra hard, seemingly embarrassed, which she would be coming directly from a workout and not feeling fresh.

I gave up trying to tell if JC was in her or not. I pinned her to the kitchen counter and shoved my tongue deep, licking her soft and sensitive inner walls. She gasped with pleasure and shifted her feet a few inches wider. I lifted her ass and burrowed my face deep, sucking and nibbling and licking until I had her on the verge of climax, but then I backed off only to bring her close again, taunting and teasing until she stomped a foot in frustration and pleaded with me to make her cum. Nope. Not yet, Bitch. Instead I stood and rammed my aching cock home. I slid all the way in, her slick, hot, tight oven enveloping me in a velvet fist. I groaned.

"You like that, you bastard?" she said. "You like that nasty pussy?"

I held her hips and fucked harder.

"I love that nasty pussy," I growled. "You must love working out. You're soaked." And then, before I could stop my stupid mouth, I said: "Did you cheat on me today? You're so wet it's like another man is already in there."

I panicked the instant those words left my mouth. What if she blurted an equally impulsive confession? For an instant I felt like I'd jumped off a cliff.

Aaliyah groaned from deep in her chest and flattened her torso on the granite counter, giving me deeper access to her cunt. She whimpered with lust, reaching back with both hands to spread her ass cheeks. The moment was intense.

I hammered her offered hole and she suddenly arched her back, crying out as a powerful orgasm shook her. I'd never made my wife cum like this and I lost my mind, roaring my delight and then ejaculating everything my nuts carried. Ali urged me on, demanding I shoot her full.

After, I we collapsed on the kitchen counter, breathing fast, sweaty, every muscle shaking. We didn't move. Eventually, Ali giggled.

"Archie better not come home," she murmured.

I chuckled.

We lifted ourselves off the marble and stood, adjusting clothing, tucking things away. Our eyes met. She took a step towards me.

"Fuck me like that any time you wish," she muttered.

I kissed her lips. I was no closer to knowing if he'd cum inside her but my blurting had added something to our mix. The idea was out there now, floating through our everyday lives. Two days later we fucked again and she was absolutely soaked once more. I made the accusing comment again although I knew there was no way she'd seen him because this time there'd been no window in her busy schedule. Her response was a wicked smile and a clenching of her vagina around my pumping dick. My shocked expression made her laugh. We kissed, in love and making love. Two days after that she brought it up during sex, which was the first time the dirty talk was her idea.

"You don't mind how wet I am?" she grunted, timed with my thrusts. "I fucked my lover again. Earlier this morning. That's him you feel."

"I love it," I said, playing along, pumping slowly.

"I thought you'd be jealous."

"I am jealous," I rumbled. "That's what makes my dick so hard."

She moaned softly.

"Don't tell me that," she said. "You'll make me want to fuck him all the time."

"Then fuck him all the time," I growled. "If it means you come home this horny and wet, fuck him all the time."

She grabbed my face and kissed me fiercely. I roughly squeezed a breast. She locked her ankles behind me and I started dropping my weight on her, pounding the woman I love.

"I feel it coming," I groaned after a while.

"Good," she teased. "Go ahead and add your load to his. Carrying more than one man inside me at the same time is hot as hell."

I went wild. I smacked her tits and she yelped. I flipped her over and drove my dick far up her pussy. I savaged her cunt, battering her into the sheets. She groaned and took it, encouraging me to punish her cheating pussy.

It was out in the open but under the umbrella of make-believe.

Dirty talk became a regular thing. We lived a lie but we loved the lie we lived. She'd come home and tell me she'd fucked someone and I'd drag her to bed. I'd stop her before she left the house, telling her she wasn't dressed slutty enough for her lover. I'd send her back to the bedroom. She'd emerge looking like a dream, taunting me about how much he was going to enjoy her looking like that.

We dug our hole deeper and deeper.

Weeks later we wandered an antique shop downtown, picking over the selection for something unique. We had a corner in the living room that needed something interesting to fill it. We shopped at the back of the store, far away from employees and other customers, when she lifted a small, hand-carved mahogany bust of Ulysses Grant, and whispered a question.

"What if I really did?" she asked.

"Did what?" I whispered back.

She held the bust in front of us, examining the intricate carved ear.

"What if I fucked someone else?"

I shrugged, playing it cool.

"I thought you already were."

"Be serious, David. Sharing fantasies is one thing but acting on those fantasies is serious. I'm asking how do you think you'd react if I did it for real?"

"We talk about it so much these days," I said, staying calm, pretending to be objective. "We toy with the idea constantly, yet our sex is better than ever. Our communication is better than ever. We feel closer and share more intimacy than ever. The idea clearly appeals to each of us. If you disclosed you truly *were* fucking someone I'd feel jealous insecurity but you could probably talk me out of that. I've pictured you stuffed with dick a thousand times already. My hurt would be more about the lie than the act, if you know what I mean."

"You wouldn't fly into a rage? You wouldn't divorce me?"

I acted like I thought I would act if I'd been completely ignorant of what she'd been doing and imaging all this for the first time. I have no idea how convincing I was.

"Is there something you need to confess, Aaliyah?"

She didn't cry. She didn't collapse. She didn't shy away from it at all. She took my hand and pulled me farther into the store and away from everyone.

"Yes, Baby," she said, voice wavering. She met my eyes.

"Go on," I prodded.

"JC," she whimpered. "I've been fucking JC."

The moment had arrived. She waited for the hammer to drop.

In an instant I decided to hide that I'd known all along. This was her confession, not mine. I was still comfortable with my lie. I'd manipulated her for the selfish purpose of better sex and that had led her to infidelity. She'd crossed the line on her own, true, but I certainly wasn't an innocent party. I needed to own my part, at least to myself.

"Is our marriage at risk?" I asked.

She recoiled in horror. Her expression told me everything.

"No!" she stated emphatically. "Never. I love you more than I ever have."

"Did you do it because something is missing in our relationship?"

"No," she said. "I did it because JC is smoking hot. My relationship with you is wonderful. I'm happily married. I didn't do it to give me something that was missing, I did it to add to all I already have. It's a form of greed. At first I was motivated by a need to know I was still attractive. But then you started suggesting I act sexier, I flirt more, I wear more revealing clothes. I know you were just trying to get me little boosts to reassure me, but one thing led to another. I got those boosts and craved more."

We studied each other.

"I have questions," I said.

"Ask them, Baby."

"Condom?"

She looked at the floor.

"No," she said.

"He cum inside you?"

She kept her eyes down.

"Sometimes," she admitted. "Most of the time."

My dick twitched in my pants. I was looking at her, remembering. She was growing sexier right before my eyes.

"Birth control?"

My throat was going dry.

"No," she mumbled.

"Why not? You want to have his baby?"

"Not at all," she said. "I feel so wild when he fucks me, so naughty. Planning for birth control would take the act out of the fantasy world and into the rational one. I always tell him to pull out but sometimes he doesn't. Also, sometimes I grab his ass and don't let him. Every time we fuck I swear it will be my last, but then I cave again."

I exhaled. That was hot. All of this was hot. Ali lifted her eyes to study me again.

"Is this turning you on?" she muttered.

I nodded, parched throat too dry to speak. Relief visibly flooded her. She placed a hand on my shoulder. She moved closer.

"I told you from the beginning how handsome he was," she said. "I warned you he was hot. Every woman at the gym wants him. They see us together and seethe. I love it. Their rage makes me wet. He strokes my ego in exactly the ways I need right now, at my age."

"That day in the kitchen. You'd just come from a workout with him. I went down on you. Do you know which day I mean?"

"Yes."

"Did you come straight home after fucking him?"

"Yes."

"Did he cum inside you that day?"

She squeezed my shoulder.

"Yes," she murmured. "I tried to stop you but you were determined. You *craved* me and I so wanted to be craved by you. Then your tongue made contact and I forgot everything except how amazing you made me feel."

She stepped back and took my hands. We were in this together, neither innocent. I was guiltier than she knew but tough shit, she was the one getting laid. I called us even.

"What now?" I asked.

She exhaled like the weight of the world had left her shoulders. She stepped close again and threw her arms around me. She squeezed.

"I don't know what's next," she said. "Strangely, now that you know, I kind of want to quit him. He was my dirty secret but he's not anymore."

I felt a strange disappointment but how could I tell her to keep fucking him?

"I have more questions," I said.

"Of course. Go ahead."

"Does he have a big dick?"

She gave me a funny look.

"Men care about stuff like that."

She looked like she was treading carefully.

"Yes."

"Does it make you cum? Do you orgasm when he fucks you with it?"

I'd shocked her.

"You really want to know that?" she asked.

"Absolutely."

"You're an odd man, David."

"Every husband would ask the same thing. Answer the question, Ali. Honestly."

"Yes, his big dick makes me cum. I cum fast and hard and always more than once. It helps that he's gorgeous and has that incredible body but Goddamn, his cock is amazing."

I took her hand and pulled her out of that store. We climbed into my convertible and I drove us to a nearby park, way in the back. The sun was setting, providing a little cover of darkness.

"What are you doing?" she asked.

I came around to her side and pulled her out of the car, bending her over the passenger door.

"Are you going to fuck me right out here?"

"Yes," I said.

I was already hard.

She looked around to make sure we were alone and then flipped her skirt over her ass. She pulled her panties down.

"Do it," she said. "Fuck me like he fucks me, like his big cock fucks me. Make me cum on yours like I do on his. You never asked if I suck his big dick. I do. I suck and I swallow. He's the first man I've ever swallowed, baby. I swallowed his load before I ever swallowed yours. Does that turn you on too?"

She was teasing me but I was encouraging it. I was behind her, unzipping and bring my erection closer. She watched me over a shoulder, talking dirty and lifting her ass anticipating penetration.

"Go on," I grunted.

"You also never asked when was our first time. I thought for sure you would. I sucked his dick the second day. I'd known him less than twenty-four hours! We left the gym together and he walked me to my car. I sat on the driver's seat and he stood close, his back against the open door. We were just talking. I pulled the front of his shorts down, shocking him and myself, and slipped his sweaty dick into my mouth. He held my head so gently. I loved it."

I shoved my dick into her steaming pussy.

"Unnngh . . . That's good, Baby. Fuck your slutty wife. He warned me when he was close but I held his hips. I was so turned on. I'd never swallowed a man before. He was my first. After that I felt I owed you."

I held her hips and hammered away, no regard for her pleasure. I needed to cum as fast as I could. I was desperate.

"Your semen tastes better than his," she said. "But he cums a lot more than you. *A lot.* I always need to gulp several times."

I groaned. She knew she was killing me.

"I'd heard horror stories growing up about the taste but those girls told me lies. Every man tastes so different. I love sucking cock. I'm thinking about adding more men to my harem."

That did it. My orgasm wasn't great but it was fast. I sprayed inside her womb and staggered away. She was quick to pull her panties up and smooth her skirt. She checked the park to make sure we were still alone. She moved close and tucked my limp penis into my pants.

"I love you," she said.

"I love you too."

"I feel so much better now that this is out in the open."

"Me too."

Not a complete truth but she was feeling such relief I was reluctant to change her understanding of our situation. A white lie, I thought, that wasn't worth correcting.

Chapter 8

Three closings in one week. This year would be one of my best. I was feeling pretty good about myself. I left my broker's office and put the top down on the convertible. I removed my tie and threw it in my briefcase.

Life was perfect.

Ali and JC were out in the open and I'd get mind-blowing sex every time she got home from a visit with him. He knew nothing of me but I knew everything about him and I found that oddly satisfying. Yes, he was fucking my wife, but somehow I still felt like I had the upper-hand.

Charlie and I spied several more times, including once when Ali took JC to the park where I'd fucked her against the car, teasing JC into fucking her the same way. She was recreating a hot scene she'd shared with her husband to see how it felt with her lover. Her orgasm was massive. That stung. Made me rock-hard, but stung.

That's the hottest thing I've ever seen, Charlie had texted. *The man's a demigod.*

I found that peculiar given that she likes women not men.

Do you wish that were you? I'd texted back.

No response. I worried that I'd offended her but she said she was fine.

So, yes, life was perfect.

I drove through the Starbucks and ordered my favorite drink. I aimed for the freeway and cruised along, smiling as the sun warmed my skin, sipping my drink.

Life *was* perfect.

Archie was on a backpacking trip with friends and gone for three days. I knew Ali and I would tear up the house, fucking everywhere. My dick tightened in anticipation. I probably had a blowjob waiting for me as soon as I got home. I stepped on the gas.

Ali uses the garage and I use the carport, so I parked and grabbed my briefcase. My key hit the lock. I entered the house calling out hello but got no response. That was not unusual. Ali might be showering or have headphones on. I headed for the master bedroom. With luck, I'd catch her naked.

I smiled again, opening the bedroom door. The big screen was on and caught my eye. On it, Ali rested on all fours, back arched, ass high. She was in the backyard and on a towel, JC behind her, holding her waist and sawing that thick cock in and out.

My jaw dropped. I'd watched this, live, on my phone weeks ago. How was it now on our bedroom television? I pulled my eyes away from the intensely erotic scene to discover Ali and JC and Charlie all leaning with backs against the headboard, watching me watch the television.

"You've been spying on me?" Ali accused.

My heart stopped. I had no words.

"All this time?" she continued. "These videos go back to the time JC visited our home to sunbathe. I realize now you set that up, manipulating me into infidelity, but for the life of me I can't understand why."

I closed my jaw. My mind raced. What the fuck had happened here?

"Why?" she asked again, the hurt in her voice obvious.

I sifted answers, deciding on the truth.

"The more turned on you are, the better sex we have," I said, realizing how awful the words were as I heard myself speak them.

This time her jaw dropped.

"You were so down on yourself," I said. "Any boost did you good. Bigger boosts made you feel even better. I spied you and Roscoe early on and wondered what you'd do if you were all alone with him. All this sprang from an innocent desire to help you. The whole thing grew organically. Before I knew it, I was putting you and JC together alone. I felt if I told you what I was doing, it would change what you did. You'd stop. You'd stay depressed."

She chewed on that. She wasn't furious or indignant. She knew she was guilty of lies and half-truths too. She was hurt that I'd deceived her and had to work through that hurt. I was wondering how everything went off the rails so easily and then Charlie slid her hand up JC's muscular thigh.

Bingo.

I'd been assassinated by a lesbian.

The man wore tight jeans and a tight T-shirt, seated between Charlie and my wife. His muscular arms ran along the headboard in either direction behind them, around their shoulders like he guarded them or perhaps they belonged to him. He eyed me suspiciously. We were meeting face to face for the first time and under horrible circumstances. He looked annoyed with me and had a right to be. True, he'd been fucking my wife and I had a right to be mad too, but to create video to watch later was just plain strange.

Thinking of video brought me back to Charlie. She nestled under his arm, unsure and anxious. Her hand crept higher and he looked down at her. Ali was still lost in thought, pondering what I'd said. Charlie moved her hand over his crotch.

"Do you want that, Little Bird?" he asked.

She nodded uncertainly, confused by her own mixed desires.

"Take it out," JC said.

I glanced at the screen to my right. JC's thick veiny cock impaled Ali. He'd sunk the thing all the way in and held it there, grinning as my wife writhed on it.

"You filmed me fucking her and started to want it too?" he asked.

"I don't know," Charlie admitted. "Maybe. I guess so. I don't want men but I want you. Nothing makes sense."

JC smiled broadly.

"You are lesbian?"

"Yeah."

"Take it out," he said again.

Ali was still unaware what transpired next to her. Charlie used both hands and trembling fingers drew down JC's zipper. The powerful masculinity of this man had seduced my wife instantly and seduced Charlie over time. She looked mesmerized as his fly opened. She wiggled fingers inside and searching, straightening him out and withdrawing him through the opening. He was a mushroom again but growing fast. She played with his dick and he turned her face to kiss. Soon his growing cock dwarfed her young hand. Her fingers looked like a child holding a Red Boa.

He aimed his hard stare at me. This threesome would be his revenge. He lifted his hips to allow more inches to emerge and Charlie held him on both palms, weighing him like a bag of rice.

"In your mouth," he said.

She froze.

No way, I thought. *No way does a gay girl willingly put a dick in her mouth.*

I was wrong. Charlie had no skill but she had desire. She wrestled with the idea a moment and then stuffed the head in, sealed her lips around the shaft and instinctively sucked hard. JC stroked her blue hair sweetly. She tried to take more, gagging and coughing while JC waited patiently.

Aaliyah finally noticed. She watched Charlie and then glanced at me for my reaction. All I did was stand and stare. I saw in her eyes that she felt this would make us even and she slipped from the bed to remove her dress and underwear. She crawled back on and added her mouth to Charlie's, sucking JC's big hairless balls.

"Let's all strip," JC said.

Ali was already nude so she stayed on the bed, watching JC and Charlie undress. Now my wife avoided my eyes. Her attention had shifted to JC and she gave him all of it. Here mouth was watering, anticipating yet another hot session with her stud. That her husband would bear witness this time only added spice.

Charlie's baggy clothes hit the floor and Lord Almighty, what a hot young body she had. Her tits were big but firm, firmer than Aaliyah's, and her ass round. Her thighs were thick and her stomach flat. She was smooth all over and I doubted she'd ever played any sport, but youth lets you get away with that. She had a three-inch scar just under her ribs and a narrow stripe of matching blue through her trimmed pubes.

Charlie avoided my eyes too. It was she that had played the tape for JC and Ali, she that had exposed our plan and turned me in, and all because she wanted to fuck JC. After filming all these weeks, she finally reached her limit and caved. I imagined the confusion the young lesbian felt left her mind spinning. The moment her sweatshirt hit the ground Charlie was on her knees stuffing JC's fat cock in her mouth again.

"You need to fuck this little darling," Ali told JC, patting Charlie on the head.

"I need to fuck you both," JC answered.

This may sound strange, but I felt enormous relief when Ali showed she was willing to share JC. It told me her connection was sexual and not emotional. Ali sat up on her knees and kissed JC on the mouth. He groped her big tits. He moved to the bed slowly, taking Charlie with him, her mouth attached to his soft cock like a lamprey. She had no idea what to do with a penis but she was improvising wonderfully. JC tried to nudge Ali onto her back but my wife shook her head.

"Her first," she said.

JC grinned and turned his attention to the younger woman. They began kissing, JC's big hands roaming her body. She was tense, anxious, worried and confused, but turned on too. He took his time, exploring slowly, giving her time to warm to her own desires. Ali moved along the bed until she was close to me.

"I get it," she murmured. "I can't be too upset because look where it led us, but I hate that you lied right to my face over and over. I know I did too, but I still hate it. Let's forgive each other and just move forward. Good?"

"Good," I said. "Should I undress?"

"So you can fuck hot young Charlie? No way in Hell."

"How is that fair?"

"I said nothing about fair. No way will I watch you with a young pretty woman like her. Nothing about this arrangement will be fair. Besides, Sweet Gay Little Charlie doesn't want you. She wants him. JC might be the only man she fucks her whole life. By the way she's handling that penis, I doubt any male has ever touched her. She's probably still a virgin. My agreement with you will be like it was. I enjoy a hot and wild fuck somewhere and then come home to another hot and wild fuck with you, but we haven't opened our marriage to other people. We've opened it to me fucking other men. At least for now. I may grow more comfortable and let you play too but we'll never be swingers. I hope you're okay with that."

What could I say? I'd thrown men at her. I shrugged my surrender.

"You get to watch in person instead of via drone," Ali said. "I'm sure the sights and sounds will be far more intense."

Charlie looked frightened but refused to release JC's dick. He explored her body with hands, fingers, lips and tongue. She was so aroused she looked like she might scream. They were posed in a sixty-nine when he eased a thick finger into her sopping pussy and stopped.

"I'll be your first?" he asked softly.

She nodded several times.

"I'm honored."

He gently nudged her thighs apart and lowered his mouth. Charlie groaned when his tongue touched her pink clit, releasing his penis for the first time to grab the back of his head. We all heard the slurping. This young thing was gushing juice, wildly turned on by her first man. Ali left my side to cross the bed on her knees, spreading JC's strong ass cheeks to lick his large hairless balls from behind. My wife reached for his hanging penis and guided it into Charlie's mouth. The young woman closed her eyes and sucked hard. Ali wet a finger and eased it through JC's sphincter, shocking the hell out of me. He moaned softly and I marveled at his self-control. I would have shot right then. Ali has never probed my anus. I wondered what additional tricks JC had taught her.

Charlie screamed in orgasm. JC's soft tongue ripped a monster climax from the girl and he carried her through it, pumping a finger slowly, teasing and coaxing her clit. Ali popped his cock from Charlie's mouth to take a turn before stuffing him back in. Charlie managed to turn her head and speak before her cheeks bulged.

"Fuck me," she whimpered. "Let me feel it."

JC rose over her, thick cock about half hard. He turned to sandwich his dick between their mouths and the women sucked him together. He grew harder by the minute. Once fully erect, he pushed my wife off his dick and crawled between Charlie's legs. Ali had wild eyes. Charlie's eyes were squeezed shut. JC nudged Charlie's legs farther apart with his brawny shoulders and then took cock in hand, placing the head at Charlie's opening.

"Your turn to sixty-nine the girl," he told Ali.

My wife moved into position, lowering her bald pussy to the young woman's mouth. This Charlie knew. Pussy she understood. She licked my wife's slit and Ali gasped. The two ladies settled into a tight sixty-nine and JC pushed Charlie's knees back, spreading her pussy. I saw my wife slather his head as much as her clit. Then his cock began to move and Charlie groaned from her soul as he filled her.

"Oh my god," she said over and over.

He encountered resistance about four inches deep but held steady pressure and soon penetrated deeper. Charlie arched her back, whimpering into my wife's pussy. Moments later Charlie howled as another orgasm ripped through her. JC chuckled.

Each time his hips pulled back I saw Ali's tongue all over his shaft and head. He'd plunge and my wife turned to licking Charlie again.

After Charlie came again, my wife lifted her face to JC.

"Take all of her," Ali said, her voice sounding a little formal.

"Take all of her," JC intoned in response.

It sounded like an inside joke, like something meaningful only to them. I was confused until I saw JC gently withdraw from Charlie's pussy and drop his cock head to rest against the young woman's sphincter. My wife returned to licking, keeping JC's head and shaft wet and slippery. Charlie moaned but lifted her legs higher and JC eased forward. The tight ring expanded to envelope his large pink head before sealing tight behind the crown. Charlie sobbed into Ali's cunt. He sank deeper and Ali licked faster. When his cock was fully embedded, Ali turned her attention to Charlie's clit, forcing an anal orgasm that seemed to destroy the younger woman.

Take all of her.

I suddenly realized JC had fucked my wife's ass too. I imagined them together, one of the recent times she'd gone to him, and JC saying he wanted to take all of her. How much convincing did she need? He probably fucked her ass all the time now, just another hole available for his delight.

My wife had passed the same experience on to Charlie.

I was stunned. My understanding of the sex between JC and Ali took a giant leap forward. Ali didn't desire JC just because he was a new lover. JC offered an entirely new kind of sex, a kind of sex she'd never experienced. My wife fucked the man like an animal. I knew in my heart he'd shot cum into every opening. She'd given herself completely to him, in all the ways a woman can give herself to a man. There had been some days she'd been with him for hours. He'd filled her with sperm in her stomach, her pussy, and up her ass all before sending her home to me.

My body went numb. Aaliyah looked like a stranger. I needed to expand my understanding of the woman, to broaden her boundaries in my head.

Strangely, my desire for her shot through the roof.

Ali left the bed to visit the bathroom but soon returned with a washcloth. JC was fucking Charlie's ass and the younger woman had her legs spread as far as she could. She rubbed her clit and mauled her tits and orgasmed yet again. Ali kissed Charlie sweetly on the mouth and then tenderly withdrew JC's stiff cock. She washed him clean and then tugged him up to their combined mouths, both women worshiping that dick with their tongues.

JC's cock looked ready to burst. I'd never seen a dick so hard. The skin was red and tight and almost see-through. Veins laced the shaft, blood pumping, head swollen. Ali pushed JC onto his back and straddled him, reaching under to guide his erection into her pussy. I saw her hole stretch tightly around his thick shaft. Charlie crawled between his legs to lick his balls and Ali's asshole as they fucked.

My legs could no longer support me. My whole body trembled. I left the bedroom for the dining room and returned with a chair, seating myself beside the bed. I had a perfect view of Charlie's big swinging tits and Ali's stuffed pussy. I wanted to masturbate but decided that would be too humiliating in front of Charlie and the man fucking my wife. Better to store every scene in my head for later. Ali knew I would fuck her to within an inch of her life when we were alone again.

After a while they all changed places again. JC fucked Charlie for a while and then moved to Ali. The women made out, exploring each other, and JC prowled around the edges, slipping his cock into any hole that appeared. I was thankful Ali's asshole was never a target. That sight would have killed me.

Finally, Charlie said she wanted JC to cum in her. He shared a glance with Ali and she gave a quick nod. Charlie rolled over onto all fours and lifted her pussy but JC flipped her onto her back.

"I want to look in your eyes when I fill you," he said.

Charlie spread her legs. JC sank his fat cock. He held out until Charlie orgasmed again and then let loose his load, filling the young woman with sperm. Everybody snuggled for a while and I thought they might be finished but I should have known better. Ali ran fingertips down his muscular arm and JC lifted his head.

"My turn," my lovely wife said.

Aaliyah rolled onto all fours like Charlie had but this time JC left her there. He pulled Charlie's mouth to his cock to get him hard and once he was, he spread Ali and sank into her steaming pussy. My wife began making the sexiest sounds I've ever heard. They moved so well together, a couple in lust, two people craving each other with all their heart. Ali soon orgasmed from his thrusting meat and then orgasmed again right away. JC pounded her hole, inching himself closer, and then shoved a thumb up her ass to hold her in place. He hammered her cunt, eager to spurt, and roared like a lion as he blasted her womb with hot sperm. He shot and shot and shot, just like he had with Charlie. Ali had mentioned JC comes a lot more than me and I saw that now and by how much.

I again made the mistake of thinking they were finished. My night lasted almost until dawn. Charlie was the first to leave, muttering something about work and that she hoped we'd still be friends. Ali and JC turned on each other like newlyweds, fucking in every position until exhaustion overtook them.

"Sometimes," Ali told me, drifting off. "I cum so hard with him he makes me cry."

Chapter 9

Come home right now, Ali's text said. *911.*

She never uses that so I turned my car to head for home. I used voice-to-text to reply: *Is Archie all right? Are you?*

We are fine, just get here.

I drove like a maniac. I parked in the driveway and ran inside. Ali sat at the kitchen table, staring at her phone. I heard video playing. She turned the phone to show me: JC and Ali fucking in our backyard.

"So?" I asked, annoyed she'd frightened me so much over a video.

"So it's from Roscoe," she snapped. "He shot this weeks ago. I'm so stupid. I forgot all about him coming to treat our pool that day with JC. He came to the gate and saw me having sex and started filming."

"Why send the video to you? I figured he'd just use it to jack off."

Her face turned red.

"You *knew*?"

"I noticed on one of the drone shots, yeah. You'd already shown him everything and more than once. Why would I worry? There was nothing to be done so I did nothing. Afterwards I forgot about him just like you."

She shook her head.

"Let me read the message that accompanied this delightful video: *Hello Mrs. Jackson. Please don't hate me for this but I'm going crazy. If you don't want this video to go to everyone in town, including your son and husband, meet me for sex this Saturday at the Motel Seven on Raintree and Collins. Eight o'clock. No condoms. I expect a yes answer before three today. I can't stop thinking about you. I must have you. I'm sorry.*"

My jaw hit the floor.

"Fucking prick," I said. "We've known him his whole life. He's spent the night with Archie a million times. We gave him his first job. What a little asshole."

"Right?" Ali cried, distraught. "What do I do? I teased him by laying out naked but I never thought it would blow up like this. Shit!"

I looked at the clock: two-forty-eight. We had twelve minutes to respond. I searched my mind but had no answers.

"Is he bluffing?" I asked. "Extorting sex is criminal. He's such a good kid. Maybe he's just trying to scare you into it."

Ali shook her head.

"We'd be risking a thousand dollars to win ten. The payoff is not worth it if we're wrong, and we'd leave him with the ability to extort me again."

We both contemplated silently.

"I'll do it," she sighed. "I'll be sweet and horny and charm him onto my side. He's young. I can manipulate him into my biggest fan. I'll rock his world and then threaten to cut him off if he ever treats me poorly again."

I had no better plan to offer. I hugged my wife. I'd expected more resistance from her but with everything else going on, what was one more lover?

She started tapping keys, speaking out loud as she wrote: "See-you-then."

She hit send.

I expected the rest of the week to drag but no, Saturday arrived like a striking cobra, here before I knew it. Ali was nervous and changed her outfit several times. She refused to look frumpy because Roscoe thought she was so hot but hated the idea of dressing sexy for him, as that would mean she'd capitulated to his evil plan. Eventually she decided on slightly sexy: knee-length white dress, tight but no cleavage, and pumps. We told Archie we were going on a date night and not to wait up for us.

Ali dropped me at an all-night bar near the Motel Seven and drove herself the rest of the way. I was almost as nervous as she. I found a booth along the back wall, ordered some food and a beer, and settled in. Roscoe had shot his load fast jerking off to Ali in our backyard, so I thought this might be a quick turnaround. I propped my phone on the table but expected no messages. I just wanted to be ready. An hour later I started checking to make sure I'd missed none. Two hours in I started to worry. No way this young man was a stud like JC. Three hours in and I paid my bill and began walking the few miles to the motel. I arrived just before midnight, sweating in the warm night air.

The place was a dive and the room easy to locate because Ali had parked directly in front of it. There was a soda machine farther down so I pretended to fish some change from my pocket and head for a drink. As I passed in front of the window I slowed my pace, eyes and ears stretched for anything. A corner of the drape was caught on the inside window sill so I lowered my eyes to look through the gap.

Roscoe and two of his friends, one black, one white, had Aaliyah sandwiched between them. My wife rode one young man while another, the black guy, fucked her ass from behind. Roscoe stood over them, feeding Ali his cock. They all moved together, intent on pleasure: their own, and what they gave. Aaliyah, her long hair snagged by the sweat on her back, moved sensuously, fucking the men deeply, sliding her tight holes up and down their rigid shafts. She gazed into Roscoe's eyes as she sucked his youthful cock, balancing one hand on the chest of the man underneath while the other teased Roscoe's balls. Movement across the room drew my eye. A fourth man sat in a padded chair, smoking a bong. He was naked and his shiny cock limp. He'd already finished fucking Ali, I surmised, and now wanted to get high. There were four of them in that room. Four.

Four.

My wife was the sexual plaything of these men in their early twenties, and she clearly loved it. The man underneath pawed her big tits. The man fucking her ass reached a hand around to grip her throat, reminding her she was a slut under their control. Ali smiled around the dick in her mouth, pleased that they were in charge.

I read the lips of the young man under her.

Can I cum inside too? he asked.

Roscoe nodded.

Yeah, he answered.

The man on his back began thrusting faster. After a minute, he lifted his ass high off the mattress, lifting Ali and the black guy with him. He dropped his hips and then thrust upward again, hard, blowing another blast of hot young sperm inside my wife.

I left the window because I had to. I'd peeped too long. I bought a soda and opened it, making the return trip slow and deliberate, pretending to study something on my phone. No one was around this time of night so I risked another look through the gap. Now three of the guys sat taking hits from the bong while Roscoe fucked Ali missionary, his white ass rising and falling slowly. Ali had drawn her legs up to his shoulders, giving Roscoe as much pleasure as she could, offering her sopping cunt completely. There was no coercion here. She smiled at him. She kissed the tip of his nose sweetly. Not exactly a woman being extorted. His ass started pumping faster but, fearing discovery, I couldn't hang around to see the climax.

It was another fifty-minute walk back to the bar but what choice did I have? She could take another three hours with that many guys and all of them young. I sipped my soda and aimed for the sidewalk. Images of Ali fucking floated through my mind.

Chapter 10

She walked into the bar two hours later. At three in the morning, I was the only patron. She did a quick scan and spotted me hiding in the back and wove between empty tables to get to me. She was twenty feet away when the smile started. She was grinning like a fool by the time she sat. The bartender looked up and I pointed at my empty beer mug and held up two fingers. He nodded and went for the tap.

"Four," Aaliyah said, suppressing a giggled.

"Four what?" I asked, playing dumb.

"There were four of them, David, all Roscoe's age. They fucked me at the same time and then took turns one after the other. My panties are holding back a flood. Young men recover so quickly."

She laughed at my face.

"I'm sorry, Baby," she said. "That was insensitive of me. I'm just giddy knowing I'm now one of those rare women who have experienced a gang bang. It thrills me to even say it. Gang bang. Not in my wildest dreams did I ever think at this age I'd finally go through one. It was exhausting but exhilarating. I'd do it again."

"You probably will."

"Roscoe showed the video of my and JC to his best friends and they all wanted to fuck me. That's how their plan hatched. They made Roscoe send me that blackmail text and then they all surprise me in the motel room. Do you have any idea how powerful a woman feels being able to satisfy four young and virile men at the same time? Fucking powerful. I made them so hard. Me. They were crazy hot for *me*. They all have girlfriends their own age but they couldn't wait to get their paws on me. You're right: I will fuck them all again."

"I saw," I said. "I walked to the motel to check on you. The curtain was snagged, open at the corner. I watched as long as I could without getting caught. I saw you."

I saw the arousal rise behind her eyes.

"You saw me fucking all of them at once?"

"Yes. You had Roscoe in your mouth, rode another guy, and the black guy fucked your ass from behind."

The bartender dropped our beers at the table so we stopped talking until he left.

"David, I had two cocks moving inside me at the same time. Three, counting Roscoe. You have no idea how hot that is. You can't imagine what that feels like. I closed my eyes and let myself experience all three simultaneously, sliding and pumping and throbbing. That was the pinnacle of my sexual life. I've never felt so feminine. I felt womanly after giving birth to Archie and being a mother but tonight I felt *feminine*. I was *filled* with hard pulsating dick. I had so many mind-bending orgasms. God! I could go back for more right now."

Listening to her I realized we weren't slowing down. We were gaining speed. I thought maybe the threesome with Charlie and JC would be some turning point, and it was, but not in the direction I presumed. Woven through my wife's excited voice I heard rising desire. She was only now beginning to understand the incredible sex life that was hers to take. All she had to do was keep going.

Chapter 11

"No," I said, flatly, easing off the accelerator. "No. Absolutely not."

"Why?" Aaliyah asked.

"Because he and his asshole friends beat me up. We should avoid that side of town entirely. He's dangerous."

Ali scooted closer, hugging my arm as I drove.

"That's what makes him exciting," she said. "It's all so wrong. He's a pig. He's a bad man from the wrong side of the tracks. My heart races at the thought of confronting him and putting him in his place."

I stepped on the gas. She says confront but I suspected she has a deeper desire, a desire hidden even from herself. I imagined Alfredo putting his hands on her and rage instantly boiled up.

"Don't be mad," she said.

"It's humiliating."

"After everything you've seen me do?"

"They beat me up and pinned me down and you want to go back to him willingly. It's demeaning."

"What do you mean: 'Going back to him?' Do you think this is a sexual thing for me?"

"I think it might be."

"Ew."

"He's hung."

"You think that's all I care about?"

"No, but I'm sure it helps. It sure held your attention that first night."

"You stared at it too," she countered. "Dicks in the wild are a rare sight."

"He'll believe you've returned because you want him."

"Who cares what he thinks?"

"I do. It's a guy thing."

"Don't be silly," she said. "You're viewing me as the prize, as a treasure to be stolen. This is between me and him, not you and him and all of them. I'm my own person just like you are. Just like he is."

I grumbled. Maybe that's how it was in woman-world but that's not how it was in man-world. Aaliyah *was* the prize. Alfredo would forever be able to gloat. True or not he'd believe Ali wanted him. If you flash your dick at a woman and she talks to you anyway, she must want you. There was no way to make Ali understand what she was doing to me in their eyes. I down-shifted the Audi and changed lanes.

"Are you taking me to him?" she asked.

"No."

"David, you can take me there right now and be a part of the conversation or I can come back without you later. I cannot let this go. Are you with me or not?"

I took my eyes off the road long enough to meet hers. She was serious.

"I know losing that fight upset you but you were outnumbered. It wasn't a fair fight. I think it's wonderful that you got out of the car to defend me. I do. You're my shining knight. But I need less defending than you think. He scared me that night. They all did. But I'm not the same woman now as I was then."

"If we go back, I'm sure there'll be another fight."

"Don't. Just stay in the car. Ignore their taunts. They're just immature boys. Let me say my piece and then we drive away."

Debate was pointless. I signaled and changed lanes again. I was convinced the encounter would not go as she predicted. No way. Not with men like that. I slowed and changed lanes again, moving over to leave the freeway. Aaliyah looked around at where we were, noting the factories and warehouse.

moment passed and she did not return. The guys started talking, chuckling at my dismay. The third guy said something and Reggie and Tall man laughed out loud.

"You nailed it, Ben," Reggie said.

More time passed.

Fredo was definitely fucking Aaliyah.

Nothing else made as much sense. How much was there to talk about? They had nothing in common. Why come back here at all? What could she possibly need to say?

Fredo was fucking Aaliyah.

The thought landed like a hammer, ringing with a kernel of truth. She may not have intended that, but by now that's what was happening. Agony tore me up. I was sure my expression gave me away. Alfredo was a dangerous creep but that danger meant excitement to Ali, and lately she had no defense against desire. She'd been so quick to leave with him, to be alone with him when the opportunity arose. My gut told me there were few reasons she wouldn't fuck the man. My mind provided torturous images of Fredo's big dark cock in Ali's grateful mouth. I shook my head.

"You know Alfredo has nine kids?" Reggie asked. "They're scattered all around town. With some rich ladies, too. There are husbands out there raising Fredo's kids for him. Mom better hope there's never a paternity test. Fredo knocks women up just by looking at them."

"A lot of rich women drive down this street?" I asked, pouring as much scorn into my voice as I could manage.

"Nah," Tall Man said. "Only you guys were dumb enough to do that. Fredo works at Red Rock Country Club. He meets them there. Hubby is golfing or making deals, neglecting his trophy wife. Fredo steps in to fill the void. He's fucked women in every room of that hotel. Now he's fucked a woman in an Audi R8 convertible coupe too."

They all had a good chuckle. I ignored them. I had no option for anger. They dropped snide comments, mostly about Fredo's sexual prowess but also reminding me how big his cock is. They made sure I knew about the times they'd watched him fuck and how wild the woman always got.

"Your girl's probably getting wild too," Tall Man said. "Right now. As I speak. Fredo is smooth. He's charming. Ladies like that."

"Arnold's speaking truth," Reggie laughed.

I refused to take the bait. They continued talking amongst themselves, loud enough for me to hear, bragging about what Fredo had done to this woman or that woman. They spent fifteen minutes on the women who they'd seen suck Fredo's cock. The man will take his dick out anywhere, it seemed. I knew they were just fucking with my head but sometimes I heard a note of truth in the tales they shared. Each time they described Fredo with a woman, I'd imagine that woman was Ali.

I glanced at my phone: fifty minutes. How could it only have been fifty minutes? My angst grew.

Eighty minutes.

An hour and forty-five.

Two hours.

Two Hours.

There was now no doubt. Alfredo and my wife was fucking at that very moment. I should be furious but I wasn't. I'd driven her here. I'd handed her over. I doubted they were still in the car. Eager to get his hands on her, Alfredo had probably taken Ali somewhere close. I pulled out my phone and checked Google Maps for nearby motels and found a place two blocks away; *The Blue Dolphin Motel.* They were there. I *knew* it. I felt it in my heart and my gut. My cheeks flushed crimson as I realized Ali probably used a credit card to pay for the room. We shared that account and that meant I also paid for the room.

I was paying for a man to fuck my wife.

I put my phone away. I'd walked the distance from bar to motel to witness Roscoe and his friends fuck Ali, but I wouldn't do that again. I couldn't bear to see him with her. Not that I had a choice. These guys would keep me here by force if necessary. But even if I could I wouldn't want to see Fredo fucking Aaliyah. I'd want to punch his arrogant, egotistical, triumphant face. Instead I squared my shoulders and stood tall, determined not to show them my anguish. Every minute was torture. She'd come back to me carrying his sperm and smiling. She'd probably have a load in her belly too. They'd been gone long enough. I pictured her tits swinging and her lovely long hair cascading down her back. I imagined the harrowing sounds of her climax, pictured her spasming cunt clamped around his thick dick. I smothered a groan.

Finally, I heard the Audi. The powerful engine echoed around the concrete canyons, drawing closer. The car turned onto our street and pulled to the curb before us, Alfredo driving. Ali had her head in his lap, sucking him like she'd sucked me that night. His dick was soft but large, bending a little at the middle as she tongued the head. His dark cock looked exhausted, fat balls resting on my car seat. He pulled his dick away from my disappointed wife and tucked it into his shorts. Ali straightened in her seat, mildly surprised to see us all standing on the sidewalk. Fredo exited the car but left it running. He tried to high-five me as he passed but I ignored him. He and his buddies laughed.

"Took it for a test drive," he gloated. "The car, too."

They all laughed again.

"Fuck off," I barked.

"You can come back any time," he told me. "If you bring Ali with you."

"We are never going to see you again," I said, dropping into the driver's seat. It was still warm from him.

He grinned smugly.

"If you don't bring her," he said. "Ali will come alone. Isn't that right, Aaliyah?"

I hated her name in his mouth. Ali looked tired and a little worn out. Her hair was messy and her top buttoned wrong. Her skirt was pushed way up her legs. I impulsively lifted the front to check for white lace panties but those were long gone. Probably in Alfredo's pocket. I shut the driver's door and Ali lowered her head to my lap, unzipping and sucking, replacing Fredo's dick with mine. The guys laughed, joking about how next time it would be their turn with my wife. I put the car in drive and pulled away, hoping to never return to this part of town, never to see Alfredo and his goons again, hoping Ali had successfully scratched the itch that nagged her.

"You were right," she said looking up from my lap. "It was a sexual thing after all."

She opened her mouth. The job she did on my dick was impressive. Her oral skills had soared over the last few weeks. She would make me cum soon so I stopped her. She sat upright, a playful, naughty smirk on her lips.

"For a woman who hates sucking dick," I said. "You've gotten really good at it."

She wiped her mouth with the back of her hand.

"Thank you," she said. "I love it now. The big ones are a challenge but that excites me more. I've discovered every man tastes different. Some taste good."

"How did Alfredo taste?"

Her eyes lit up.

"Alfredo tasted great. JC not so good. Too much protein. Roscoe was delicious. I actually enjoyed his. I'll suck off that young man anytime he wants."

"Where do I fall on your semen flavor chart?"

She rested her head on my shoulder.

"More towards the bad end," she said. "Sorry, Baby."

I made a few turns and merged onto the highway, heading for home.

"Tell me everything," I said. "What happened after you left with him?"

"Are you sure you want to hear that? I know how much you hate the man. I figured you'd let sleeping dogs lie."

"You're my wife. I need to know. I can never have a man knowing something about you that I don't."

"Fair enough," she said. "His hand went under my skirt the moment I pulled away from the curb. He fondled my pussy, teasing me. He said I was already soaked which surprised me. I swear I had no plans for anything sexual but his bold move turned me on. He knows how to handle a pussy. His softly stroking fingers made up my mind. I'd expected him to be rough and clumsy but he was tender and gentle."

"His thugs say he's a ladies' man."

"I believe it. He was instantly in charge. I asked him where we were going and he directed us to a motel close by. They knew him there. I paid for a room and he put his arm around my shoulder as we walked the long hall. He's uneducated but he's not stupid. He's got a quick wit."

"And a big dick."

"Yes," she said. "There is that. His body has many scars: knife and bullet holes. He's had a hard life but he loves women."

We shared a quiet moment.

"Why him?" I asked, still disbelieving Ali picked such a man.

She thought for a moment, selecting her words carefully.

"I started thinking about finding my own man weeks ago. You choose JC for me. Roscoe was a forced choice, although I enjoyed it. Alfredo, I picked for me. I liked that he was a man nobody would ever imagine me with. I liked that he's a world away from me and my soft, convenient, comfortable life. I liked his criminal element and dangerous aura."

"Did he fuck you?"

She leaned her back against the passenger door.

"Baby, he fucked the soul out of me."

"Show me your pussy."

She looked alarmed for a split second and then adjusted her knees. She pinched the hem of her denim skirt and slowly lifted, teasing me with what I was about to see. I punched the light button on her side of the console and there she was: her swollen, pink, battered pussy. My throat constricted imagining his cock had been in there minutes ago.

"He came inside you?"

Her face softened.

"Why in the world would you ask questions like this? I can see in your eyes how they upset you. Why hurt yourself?"

"I don't know why, but I need to know. I must know what happened, the truth, without you keeping anything from me."

"All right."

I settled into the fast lane, eyes staring straight ahead.

"He removed my panties in the hallway," she began. "Before we ever made it to the room. He stuffed them in his pocket and slipped a hand under my skirt from behind. He fingered me as we walked, smiling as other people walked by. I was mortified but it also turned me on. He stopped well before our room and leaned against the wall, telling me to take his cock out and suck it in public. I refused, humiliated, but he just waited for me, smiling that dangerous little smirk of his, like he knew my desire would eventually overcome my reluctance. He was right. I knelt and obeyed, blushing like crazy as people passed and saw me with his dick in my mouth. I felt like a cheap whore but God, I got so wet."

She squirmed in the passenger seat, remembering.

"He pulled my skirt up in back so high my butt cheeks showed. He pushed my mouth away and walked the remaining distance to our room with his cock out and swinging. People turned as we passed, checking out my ass. I knew they could see my bare pussy from behind and that turned me on too. I sucked him again as we stepped into our room and locked the door. I was a little frightened to be alone with this dangerous stranger but I felt so wild I didn't care. I wanted to suck him off and drink his load but he made me stand and strip, saying high-class women like me were his favorite kind of bitches."

She held up her hand, fingers shaped into a C.

"He's this big around, Baby. Trust me, that big around feels like a tree trunk sliding in. He walked me backward until the bed hit behind my knees and then laid me down on my back. He told me to hold my legs open and I did but he told me to spread them wider. I moved my hands to my ankles and pulled. I could have died from shame spreading myself like that to a man like him. He smirked and moved closer. I lifted my head to look down my stomach at him between my legs, cock in hand. The moment was surreal. I don't even know him! He placed the fat head at my opening and gently pushed, telling me to keep my legs wide open. I would have anyway but it was hot to do it for him. He's so thick he began to sink in like I'm made of creamy peanut butter. My walls opened before his invading cock head, pushing me apart, slowly sinking deeper. He's bigger around than JC and I thought JC would kill me the first time I took him."

"JC feels good?"

"JC feels *amazing* but Fredo feels even better. Girth is the best part of a man's cock but I was also blown away to be under this man. Before tonight I never would have fucked a man like Fredo. Never. Then I found myself gazing up at his face over me and feeling his fat cock moving inside me and my mind did somersaults. I pulled my ankles back to give him everything, to open myself completely to him. He understood and grinned, telling me he would fill my pussy with his load."

She lifted her skirt to look at her abused pussy.

"I came so fast, Honey," she continued. I came when he said those words and I came again as soon as he got it all the way in. I squeezed my pussy around him. Crazy tingles started at my clit and spread, locking my hips. He laid his body atop mine and his weight pushed me into the bed. I felt trapped, his stiff cock probing deep inside me. I came all over him again, screaming. After that he flipped me over and fucked me from behind. He pushed a thumb up my ass and rested his chin on my neck, whiskers scratching my skin. I came then too."

She eased a finger into her tender pussy, probing as I drove in the night.

"I told him I wanted to ride him but he refused saying I hadn't earned that privilege yet, saying I could be on top next time but tonight was all about him taking me. His sexism got me hot and I hated myself for it. His hard cock kept plunging into me and I wished for it to never end. I knew nothing except his fat dick in me. I felt slutty and reckless. I came again. He rolled me face up and shoved his dick deep. He felt like iron. I had him so excited and that excited me. He fucked me like that slow and strong and I came *again*, pounding the sheets with a fist. He slowed way down, torturing my stretched pussy throughout my orgasm."

She thoughtfully withdrew the finger from her pussy and showed me his semen in the dome light.

"He pumped a flood into me, Baby," she admitted. She stuck the messy finger in her mouth. "I was so hot for it and wrapped my arms and legs around him and wouldn't let go. I hugged him like I was trying to squeeze the sperm out of him. He erupted like a volcano, trembling and convulsing as he exploded in my pussy. I may have wept a little, it was all so intense."

She slipped her shiny finger into her mouth, rolling her tongue around.

"We stayed in that position a long time, resting, feeling our bodies pressed together. He was still in me but softer. He filled my tunnel and my pussy just hugged him like a friend. After that he left the bed and sat in a dining chair. I knelt between his legs to play with his spongy cock and he responded, getting hard again fast. I straddled his lap and he guided my hips down. We both stared at his upright missile drawing closer and I giggled. It was a delightful sight. He was shiny from my pussy juice and getting closer every second. He pierced me, spreading my pussy lips out of the way and I relaxed my legs, letting my weight push me down onto him. We kissed, fucking face to face again, and I fed him my tits from time to time. I also reached around to play with his big balls. When he said he was getting close I rode him harder and faster. I wanted him to cum in me again. I knew almost nothing about the man yet I would take his load? God! Thinking about it turns me on again. Did you make me stop sucking your dick because you're taking me home to fuck me to death?"

I shook my head. Disappointment filled her eyes.

"Archie's home," I said. "I'm taking you to a hotel to fuck you to death."

Her eyes danced with joy.

"Or maybe I'll find a handsome stranger in the hotel bar and he can fuck you to death."

She bit her bottom lip.

"Don't pick someone you think I'd like," she said. "Pick someone you want to see fuck me. Don't ask for my input at all or try to guess what I'd like. Find a man and order me to fuck him. Pick some guy I'd never pick and give me to him."

Hot idea, but for another night. Tonight, she was filled with Alfredo and I wouldn't do that to an unsuspecting man. I'd do it to myself, though.

I got us a room and fucked her to exhaustion. There is nothing in life that prepares you for pushing your hard dick into your wife and the swirl of another man's sperm already in there. I was mildly disgusted but wildly turned on. Aaliyah murmured further details of her time with Fredo and I had to hold back my climax like a lion tied with a string. I wanted to cum so badly but I wanted to hear everything she had to say. She warned me she'd see him again. She admitted she'd given him her cell number and permission to send her dick-pics.

"In time," she'd breathed hotly in my ear. "I'll guide his thick cock up my ass. It's inevitable."

Yeah, that was when I shot my load.

Chapter 12

I moved silently through the dark apartment, ugly shag carpet beneath my feet. Ali was in here, somewhere, moving from room to room and man to man. I discovered Ben asleep atop his covers, nude, deflated cock already drained. I moved down the hallway. At the next bedroom, I found Arnold. He lay atop the covers too but with eyes wide open.

"She's been here and gone," he said, tired. "She's a lioness."

I'd become aware of Ali's devious plan gradually. I questioned my wife on her intentions but she stayed quiet. She believed she couldn't tell me her goals without emasculating me so I was left to watch them unfold.

Ali had visited Fredo's apartment four times since the night she drove away with him and each time Fredo's goons had hit on her behind Alfredo's back. No honor among thieves.

"You will cause a huge problem if you fuck any of Alfredo's guys," I'd told her.

"Men are absurd," she'd said. "You don't own the woman once you fuck her. She's still her own person and can make her own choices."

"All that is true," I'd said. "But that's how we think. If you fuck any of Fredo's guys, you'll start a war between friends."

She'd smiled.

"I know what I'm doing," she'd said.

I was showing homes when her text arrived.

I'm going to Fredo's, she'd written. *Time to start a war.*

This surprised me. I knew from an earlier conversation that Fredo wasn't home right now. Fredo had gotten arrested for burglary two days ago and was still waiting for paperwork to process before he was released on bail. Why go to his place when he's not there?

I finished with my client and drove across town. I knew where he lived because I'd dropped Ali here her first visit. Driving away had been one of the most difficult things

I'd ever done. I'd driven the parking lot until I'd found our Audi and parked several spots away. I'd entered the unlocked apartment and begun my search.

I left Arnold and continued down the hallway. The door on my left was ajar so I silently nudged it open, first noticing Ali's purse on the dresser. The door swung wider.

Reggie was on his back as Aaliyah rode him, her spread ass aimed at the door. His ugly cock sliced in and out like a piston, large head stretching her hole before plunging deep again. The semen of the men before him coated his dick. He tried to pull her face down for a kiss but she refused.

"Just fuck me," she exhaled. "Try to make it last this time."

My eyebrows rose.

"Sorry," Reggie mumbled. "You're just so hot."

"Bullshit," Ali gasped between thrusts. "You're just thrilled to be fucking Fredo's woman. Now fuck me like you mean it."

Reggie began driving his hips skyward. Ali fed him a hanging tit, her words ringing in my ears: *Fredo's woman.* Is that who she was? Can she be my loving devoted wife and Fredo's woman?

Before I could answer my own question, I heard the front door slam. Reggie and Ali did not. They were too busy fucking like animals. Heavy footsteps thundered down the hall. I stepped into the room, gliding behind the door to hide.

"You motherfucker!" Fredo bellowed moments later.

The boss man burst through the door and headed for the bed. Ali jumped off Reggie's dick, smoothly stepping aside as Fredo went for Reggie. She watched the first blow land: Alfredo's heavy fist squarely on Reggie's jaw. She stepped back as the men tangled, fists flying, angry shouts filling the room. Now I understood her plan. Now I saw the insidiousness.

I gripped her purse quietly and then gently took her elbow. She was startled to find someone behind her and even more shocked to learn it was me. I placed a finger to my lips and backed her into the corner with me as Arnold came down the hall and into the room. He immediately joined the fight but on Reggie's side. Civil war.

I tugged Ali out of the room.

"My dress!" she hissed.

"Leave it," I whispered harshly. "I'll give you my jacket."

We hurried from the apartment. I returned her purse to her and she slipped my sports coat on. She fished out her car keys.

The boom of a gunshot roared through the apartment. I looked shocked but Ali only grinned.

"We've got to leave," I stated. "Right now."

She nodded and followed me out the front door.

"Teach them to lay hands on my man," she muttered as we raced across the lawn. "Nobody gets away with that."

"You set them at each other for beating me up?"

"Yes," she replied, cold as ice. "After I got what I needed from Fredo I knew it was time. I had no idea one of them would have a gun and use it. I wonder who got shot?"

I was stunned but saved it for later. For now, we ran to our cars. My sports coat billowing, exposing her naked and freshly fucked body to the apartment complex. I was sure witnesses would describe Aaliyah to the police but what could they do? This rundown place had no security cameras.

We climbed in our cars.

"See you at home," I said.

Ali grinned: gorgeous, half-naked, and more ruthless than I'd ever imagined. I felt a strange pride that she'd brought that gang down for me.

Before we left the parking lot, I heard two more gunshots. Curious neighbors began to emerge from their apartments. A forth gunshot echoed through the complex.

I'd read in the news tomorrow about the deaths of two known gang members and the arrests of two others, Alfredo and Ben, but for now I drove cautiously and carefully, avoiding attention.

Alfredo would get eight years. His lawyer successfully worked in an element of self-defense. He'd be out in four for good-behavior. Ben had the deaths pinned mostly on him and had to serve twelve.

Ali would meet Fredo at the prison gate the day he was released and explain the guys had forced themselves on her. He bought it because he wanted to believe it. She drove him back to our place and with Archie away at college, fucked the man in our marital bed. I watched and then joined in.

I was holding her butt cheeks wide open when his well-lubed cock penetrated her ass. She'd said it was inevitable and she was right. Ali came so hard I thought my wife would lose her mind. He fucked her like a bad man because he was one, whispering in her ear how he killed two men for her. Creepy, yeah, but Ali orgasmed like a volcano. Her bad boy was an authentic bad boy and nothing made her hotter. I was eating her empty pussy when she came, her ass filled with thick hard cock. I worried she might die. He ejaculated soon after, exploding deep inside, master now of every hole.

I decided to save my climax for later, after his departure. Let them have each other fully tonight. The man had a lot of years to make up for so I excused myself and slept on our couch. He fucked her all night, sweet cries of feminine pleasure drifting through our home.

I'd hated her decision to fuck that man that beat me up but I hated it less now. My understanding had grown about why she needed it to be him. In a way, it was more exciting. He'd conquered me and claimed my woman and my woman was thrilled that he had. The whole thing was wonderfully complex and I decided not to solve it and just go with the flow. He pushed Ali's buttons. That was all I needed to know.

JC moved on to the next married woman and Charlie fell in love with the pretty girl that dyed her hair. She kept our secret and never told Archie. I still use her to take pictures of homes and she sometimes asks about JC.

Perhaps I should arrange another threesome.

End